Earthbound Angel
Catherine George

Harlequin Books

TORONTO • NEW YORK • LONDON
AMSTERDAM • PARIS • SYDNEY • HAMBURG
STOCKHOLM • ATHENS • TOKYO • MILAN
MADRID • WARSAW • BUDAPEST • AUCKLAND

ISBN 0-373-03420-2

EARTHBOUND ANGEL

First North American Publication 1996.

CHAPTER ONE

It was hot. Summer had arrived at last, sudden and sweltering, and Imogen welcomed it after the chill of a long, wet spring. But her welcome was a shade too warm, she thought, panting and breathless with exertion. A pity June hadn't waited until she'd mown the lawn before flaming into the high eighties.

Gardens were very different in practice from in theory. In their pretty London town house the walled patio had been the nearest thing to a garden she'd known until Philip had decided that they needed a weekend place in the country. Brought up in London, in a house with no garden at all, she'd yearned for apple trees and lawns starred with daisies. Now they were hers with a vengeance, and the cottage that went with it.

But the sale had gone through in early autumn, when the garden had been neatly subsiding into winter hibernation. The estate agent had rhapsodised on the glories it would reveal come spring. And he had been right. Imogen had been charmed when fat white cushions of snowdrops were duly succeeded by serried ranks of daffodils, then, joy of joys, by bluebells in the wild, woody corner of the garden—the garden which now threatened to take over her life.

Perspiring, she thrust the machine down the last strip of lawn and switched it off with a sigh of relief, shook the last grass clippings on to the compost heap and put the mower away in the shed. On her way back to the house she scowled at the herbaceous borders. Unlike the well-behaved beds of her dreams these seemed to sprout weeds overnight. Yellowing spears of daffodil leaves sprawled everywhere, her roses needed spraying, the lupins were covered with some horrible blight and slugs were devouring the delphiniums.

Suddenly overwhelmed by it all, Imogen slumped down on the rustic wooden bench that Philip had bought on the day he'd signed the contract for the cottage. At the thought of him grief and anger surged up in unison, and for a minute or two she battled hard against her familiar arch-enemies.

What she needed, she told herself firmly, was a bath and a walk. The weeding could wait until evening when it was cooler. Instead she'd walk to the village post office and put a card in the window—advertise for someone who could spare a few hours a week to work in the garden. The restoration work was almost finished on the house, but the garden needed attention urgently in order to appeal to a prospective buyer. It was becoming increasingly obvious that she must sell the house. If Philip had been here with her she would have tried to settle to life in a country village, to become part of the community. But on her own it was a mad idea to live in a listed cottage at the end of a no-through road miles from anywhere.

To soothe her sorely tried muscles Imogen lay for a while in her claw-footed Victorian tub, then dried herself briskly and treated her sun-flushed skin to the expensive lotion that Philip had liked so much. Her

wide, full mouth tightened. Philip. Everything she did
came back to him.

She sighed and went into the adjoining bedroom.
It was dominated by a wide bed with a headboard
painted with pre-Raphaelite angels whom she eyed
malevolently. Philip had found the headboard in an
antiques shop and paid the earth for it, unaware that
angels were not her personal cup of tea at all, particularly now that he had deserted her company for
theirs.

In this room it was harder to get away from his
presence than anywhere else in the cottage. Which was
strange. Illogical. A day or so at a time was all they'd
ever spent together here. She'd simply sold her one-
bedroom flat and moved into Philip's smart North
London town house when they married. Very little of
her own personality had been stamped on it.

Yet here in Beech Cottage, in this room where she'd
chosen most things herself—barring the angel headboard—she felt haunted by him, missed his restless,
vital presence. Her face burned suddenly. If she was
honest she missed him in that great lonely bed at times,
even now, and the knowledge fuelled anger again.
Anger unbecoming for a grief-stricken widow.

She brushed her hair furiously to banish the
thought, caught her long, red-brown hair back at the
nape of her neck, added a few touches of make-up
to her tanned face, and regarded the result with wry
disillusion. The colour of rain-wet moss, Philip had
once described her eyes. But that was before they had
reddened with weeping when he died. She eyed her
reflection militantly. No more weeping and wailing.

Instead she'd concentrate on getting help. Otherwise she'd need a physiotherapist far more than a gardener.

In deference to the hot, sunlit day, Imogen took a dress from the wardrobe—fine, diaphanous cotton with a dense print of ochre and white flowers on a brown background. As the fabric slithered softly against her skin she realised that it was a long time since she'd worn a summer dress, or any dress at all. Tailored shirts and trousers, and, in more relaxed mood, heavy sweaters and jeans were all she seemed to live in. But today was definitely a day for a change.

Outside, the noon sun was blowtorch-hot and Imogen hastily retreated indoors for a hat—the straw hat that Philip had bought her in Venice. *Stop* it, she told herself fiercely. All this haunting by her husband just couldn't go on. Widow's weeds were no longer fashionable, particularly when the widow was a mere thirty-two years old. Imogen swallowed. Thirty-two! Where had the past ten years gone?

But the past was over. Her priority was to find a way to get through the next ten, and find it fast. Moping the hours away at Beech Cottage was the last thing that Philip would have wanted. Damn! There I go again, she thought angrily.

Settling the wide-brimmed hat over her eyes, Imogen locked the kitchen door and set off down the path to the gate, breathing in summery scents from the fields and hedgerows on either side of the lane. She walked at a leisurely pace along a cathedral-like arch of green trees only recently come into full leaf, glad of the shade as she made a mental list for the village shop.

The post office store in Abbots Munden was a surprisingly large establishment, and due to enthusiastic support from the residents stocked such a wide range of goods that Imogen rarely bothered to venture further afield for supplies. The shop was fairly crowded when she went in. Returning the usual, carefully friendly smiles, she took a wire basket and helped herself to salad greens, Jersey potatoes, some ripe peaches and a loaf of crusty, seeded bread. Mr Jennings, the proprietor, cut her a few slices from a succulent ham and gave her a bit of strong, ripe farmhouse cheese to taste as she pondered her choice from the others in his impressive selection.

'Actually, Mr Jennings, I was hoping you'd be able to help me,' she said, adding a bag of apples to her spoils as he cut her a wedge of single Gloucester.

'Only too glad to, if I can,' he assured her.

Imogen explained about her burgeoning garden and her own inadequacy in dealing with it. 'I was hoping you might know someone who could put in a few hours for me, or, if not, can I leave a card in your window?'

'Do that by all means,' he said quickly, then thought for a moment. 'Though, if you go home the long way round, by Mill Lane, you'll pass Camden House. The Sargent place. Mrs Sargent's in America visiting her daughter, but Sam Harding helps in her garden. He's usually there this time of day. Perhaps he could give you a hand. If not get back to me and I'll ask around.'

Imogen thanked him warmly, gave a farewell smile to everyone in general and went outside. The afternoon sun lit up Abbots Munden like a film set. The village, tucked away in a remote fold in the

Cotswold hills, was remarkably unspoilt. Most of its honey-coloured buildings dated from the mid-sixteenth to the mid-seventeenth century, and instead of the usual village pond a tributary of the River Leach ran through the village, broad and shallow, with an occasional footbridge to add to the general photogenic quality.

Yet so far, owing to its distance from even the newest of motorways, Abbots Munden managed to avoid the tourist-weary look of some of the more commercially popular beauty spots in the area. The remains of a Norman motte-and-bailey castle stood right in the middle of clustering cottages and houses, and in the church several Norman features had survived the Victorians' zeal for restoration.

Camden House stood behind walls just beyond the church. Imogen turned in through the gates and crunched her way along the white gravel of the drive which led to a house very like many of the smaller ones she'd passed on her way through the village. This one was larger, more irregular in shape, but with the same typically prominent gables and low, steeply pitched roof.

Moulded drip-courses crowned windows wreathed by a gnarled old wisteria which joined a climbing, creamy yellow shower of roses. In the herbaceous borders tall lupins in shades of pink and purple and cream stood like guardsmen among the dwarf sweet-williams and cape daisies blooming in a riot of pink and white.

Imogen stared at the garden, depressed. The lawns looked like stretches of green velvet, and if there was a weed anywhere she couldn't spot it. But there was no sign of the artist who presided over all this perfection.

A gate set in a stone archway obviously led to more gardens at the back of the house. Imogen hesitated, then, spurred on at the thought of her own chaotic garden, pushed the gate open and went through into another paradise of manicured lawn giving on to a tennis-court bordered by shrubs and trees which screened a vast vegetable garden where someone was working.

Her eyes brightened. Feeling like a trespasser, she crossed the lawn and skirted the tennis-court to venture through a rose-covered arbour which led through into the kitchen garden. A man was digging energetically behind a row of poles where runner bean plants would climb later on.

He was younger than expected. Stripped to the waist, his brown torso gleamed with sweat in the sunshine as he dug a trench with a speed and expertise she envied. This man so very obviously knew what he was doing. His longish hair glistened black and curly in the sunshine above the red bandanna tied round his forehead, and he wore tattered jeans and mountain boots, and earth-encrusted gardening gloves.

Imogen coughed but the man took no notice, too absorbed in his labours to hear. She called, 'Hello there!' but there was still no response. Then she realised that the scarf hid two earphones and saw a lead running down the man's back to the Walkman radio tucked into the pocket of his jeans.

She dumped her basket down on the path and trod gingerly along the hard-packed earth bordering the trench until she came into the gardener's line of vision. The man shot upright in surprise, his eyes widening at the apparition before him—at the wide straw hat, dark glasses, filmy dress floating on the light summer breeze. She smiled at him, hoping that she didn't look as astonished as she felt. She'd been prepared for a weather-beaten, elderly man. This man was tall and muscular and young, his dark eyes gleaming with open appreciation for a second before he hastily pulled off a glove and switched off his radio.

'Mr Harding?' said Imogen hopefully.

'Afraid not.' The man smiled, his teeth white in his dark, perspiring face. 'Sam's hurt his hand. I'm filling in for him for a while—under strict instruction,' he added. 'Can I help?'

Imogen smiled ruefully. 'I was told Mr Harding might spare me a few hours' work at my place—the garden's getting badly out of hand, however much I slave away in it. I'm in desperate need of some expert advice—but I'm obviously out of luck. You wouldn't know of anyone who might help?'

'*I* could,' offered the man after a pause. 'I'm not expert exactly, but I've done plenty of gardening in my time. I could tidy your place up for you on a temporary basis—put in a week or so's work until you find someone else, if you like.'

Imogen gave him a smile radiant with gratitude. 'Would you? That's wonderful, Mr . . . ?'

'Gabriel.'

'Right. When could you start, Mr Gabriel?'

'Tomorrow? And just Gabriel will do.'

'Tomorrow would be fine—Gabriel. I'm Imogen Lambert,' she added. 'I live at Beech Cottage at the end of Glebe Lane.'

She saw his face alter, as she'd known it would. In a village like this everyone probably knew about her. And her situation.

'How do you do, Mrs Lambert?' he said gravely. 'I heard about your husband. I'm very sorry.'

She was taken aback by his condolences. Most people avoided the subject like the plague. 'Thank you. Tomorrow morning, then—about nine?'

'On the dot,' he said promptly, and smiled again, dispelling the slight awkwardness.

Quelling an impulse to shake hands, she smiled back, said goodbye, then retraced her steps along the bean row to her waiting basket, aware that a pair of bright, narrowed eyes watched her out of sight as she retreated through the rose arbour and hurried across the lawn to the side-gate.

On the walk home Imogen's spirits were higher than they'd been for some time, which was simply because she had an offer of help with that jungle of a garden, she assured herself. The fact that the help came in the shape of a young Adonis like Gabriel was nothing to do with it. Well, not much, she thought with a grin. Now that the workmen had finished on the interior of the cottage the peace and quiet was hard to bear at times. The prospect of another human being in the vicinity every day was very welcome. Whatever his age.

As she went through the door into the kitchen the telephone was ringing. She snatched it from the wall and beamed with pleasure at the sound of a familiar voice.

'Tash! How did it go?'

'Let's just say it went,' said her stepdaughter, chuckling. 'Never mind, that's my first year in college under my belt—and I think the exams were OK actually, Stepmama, so you can uncross your fingers. How are you?' added Natasha Lambert in a different tone.

'Rather pleased with myself,' said Imogen lightly. 'By my standards I've had quite an exciting day. I mowed the lawn, walked into the village to the shop, and, best of all, I managed to acquire the services of a gardener for a week or so to get this place into shape. You should *see* it right now—the garden from hell!'

Tash laughed, then, after a pause, said, 'Um—look, love, there's something I want to ask.'

Imogen's lips twitched. 'There usually is.'

'Are you all right? Really, I mean?'

'Yes,' said Imogen, eyes narrowed. 'I really am, Tash, so ask away.'

'Well, you know I was coming to you next week for a bit, after my visit to the grandparents?'

Imogen's heart sank. 'Yes. Go on.'

'Would you mind awfully if I didn't for a couple of weeks? Steph's asked me to go on holiday to France—don't worry, not on our own. Her family take this farmhouse in the Périgord every year, and this time—because of Dad and everything—Mrs Prescott asked if I'd like to go too. Grandma's happy as long as you are,' added Tash breathlessly, and Imogen laughed.

'Of course I don't mind. I admit I panicked at the back-packing Himalayan idea, but France with the Prescotts sounds ideal. How about clothes?'

'Grandma's roped her daily in to do my washing— a one-off treat for the weary student, I hasten to add. And if I dash up to you on Saturday could you possibly sort out any casual stuff I left with you? I rather fancy my passport's hanging round somewhere in the cottage too.'

Imogen gave assurances that she'd do whatever was necessary, and after Tash rang off congratulated herself on hiding her own disappointment.

Natasha Lambert had been twelve years old when Imogen first met her, and they'd taken to each other from the start. Tash, motherless from infancy, had been gratifyingly delighted when Philip told her that Imogen had agreed to marry him. And it was Tash who flew to Imogen's side when Philip died. They'd suffered their loss and grief together.

Now, almost a year later, Natasha was recovering well, helped by the resilience of youth, her studies at university, and the love and support of her mother's parents, Henry and Barbara Foster. Imogen's recovery had been slower. But in some undefined way today had been a turning-point. Whether it was the sunshine, or the promise of a helping hand, she felt suddenly optimistic—even in firm control of the anger which still smouldered below her grief over Philip's death.

Imogen was finishing the contents of the coffee-pot over the morning paper the next day when a knock on the kitchen door heralded Gabriel's arrival. She let him in, wondering how one proceeded in the circumstances. With the hired help did one ask him to sit down and drink a cup of coffee, or did one offer him one out in the garden where he wouldn't feel obliged to make conversation? For a start, Gabriel was a pretty far cry from her idea of a jobbing gardener, one way and another. His speech not only lacked the lovely local burr but hinted at pursuits a lot less leisurely than horticulture. And now that she saw him again she had no doubt at all that he was a star turn with the opposite sex too.

This morning he wore the same clothes as the day before, with the addition of a faded rugby shirt and a faint look of surprise.

'Is something wrong?' asked Imogen when the morning greetings were over and the usual comments made on the wonderful weather.

He shook his head. 'No. It's just that you look different without the hat and sunglasses—Mrs Lambert,' he added belatedly.

Not sure what he meant by this, she offered him coffee.

'Not at the moment, thanks. I'd like to get on before it gets too hot. They've promised a scorcher today.' He frowned suddenly. 'I forgot to ask. Do you have any garden tools?'

She laughed. 'You mean you took one look at the garden and decided I don't have any at all!'

Gabriel grinned. 'Not exactly. But if you're new to gardening it struck me that you might lack a few essentials.'

'Fortunately we bought all the stuff belonging to old Mrs Driver, the former owner. And my husband added a few more bits and pieces.' She turned away to clear the table. 'I'm afraid the lawnmower's past its first youth, but I think you'll find most of the usual things in the garden shed.'

'Right. I'll make a start. Is there anything in particular you want done first?'

She smiled at him over her shoulder. 'The beds bordering the lawn are bothering me most because I can see them from the sitting-room window. Oh, and some peculiar white insects are crawling over the lupins—' She shuddered. 'Not to mention the slugs dining off my delphiniums!'

'A bit of spraying first on the agenda, then.' He indicated the rucksack he'd dumped down by the kitchen door. 'To save time I brought a couple of things, spray and sprayer included.'

'How forward-thinking!' said Imogen, and bit her lip, realising too late that she might have sounded patronising. 'Right, then—Gabriel. If there's anything else perhaps you'd make a list for me and I'll go shopping in Cheltenham.'

He looked at her for a moment, then nodded. 'Fine, Mrs Lambert. Is the shed locked? Perhaps you'd come with me to take an inventory?'

Inventory? Did he think she doubted his honesty? Trying to think of some way to assure him that she didn't, she walked ahead of him down the garden path, suddenly sorry that she was wearing much washed jeans which fitted her rather too well. Not that young Gabriel would be interested in her back view, of course, but to her annoyance her flustered feeling intensified once they were inside the garden shed.

It was small and rather dark with only one small, cobwebby window and a couple of shelves ranged with various canisters and cans, as well as the usual array of hoes, rakes, spades, forks and trowels, some of which were new. There was an ancient wheelbarrow, a watering-can, the petrol-driven lawnmower, a strimmer that she was too nervous to use, a couple of cans of petrol and one of motor oil, plus piles of earthenware plant pots.

'Well?' said Imogen, pulling a face. 'Will this do for a start?'

'Better than I expected,' said Gabriel, who was of necessity standing so close in the confines of the shed that the scent of young, clean male flesh flustered her still further. 'In fact,' he added, waving a hand at one of the canisters, 'you've got some of the spray I need, though I don't see anything to spray with, so it's just as well I brought something along.'

'Did you borrow it from Mr Harding?' she asked, escaping out into the sunshine.

'No. I had one of my own.' Again the white smile in the tanned, good-looking face. 'It's only a bit of plastic, Mrs Lambert. No big deal. I'll leave it with you when I go so that you can spray regularly.'

'Regularly?' She stared at him in dismay. 'Oh, dear. I thought you'd just spray once and that was that. No more creepy-crawlies.'

He shook his head and stripped off his shirt, draping it over a rickety, folded deckchair. 'Gardening's a rewarding pastime, Mrs Lambert, but it's hard, repetitive grind as well. Boring, too.'

Averting her eyes from his admirable musculature, she hurriedly showed him the outside water tap so that he could make up the spray solution, waved a rather embarrassed hand towards the outhouse lavatory, then retreated indoors.

While she was tidying the house she found herself taking frequent peeps out into the garden. Gabriel, having sprayed the lupins, roses, and a few other plants which she hadn't realised needed the same attention, was now getting to grips with the weeding, earphones tied firmly in place with the familiar red bandanna as he worked.

Suddenly she bit her lip in consternation. She'd forgotten to ask how much he charged. What a moron! He probably thought of her as a clueless townie who had no idea what wages people usually asked. He'd hold her to ransom, of course. His 'a week or so's' work until she found someone else would probably cost the earth. She laughed suddenly. Which was very apt since he was digging in the stuff right now.

When she took him his coffee she'd get things clear. Ask him what he expected to be paid. And if that differed from her own idea of a fair wage she'd tell him straight that she'd manage without his efforts. Somehow.

Imogen marched across the lawn at precisely eleven o'clock and tapped the oblivious Gabriel on his bare brown shoulder. He leapt to his feet, stripping off his gloves to switch off his radio, slanted dark eyebrows raised in enquiry.

'I have a question, Gabriel,' she said baldly. His eyes, she saw at close range, were a smoky grey which grew visibly smokier at her manner.

'Fire away.'

'Because I'm new to this sort of thing I should have brought the subject up first,' she went on crisply.

'Do you mean references?' he said quickly.

She looked blank. 'No. Since you were working for Mrs Sargent I didn't consider that necessary. What I meant was that I didn't ask what you charged.'

Strong white teeth caught in his lower lip, Gabriel stared down at the section of border he'd cleared, then mentioned the sum Sam Harding was paid by the hour. 'Of course I wouldn't expect as much as that,' he went on, 'because my labour isn't as skilled as his. So if I charge about half of what he gets would you consider that fair?'

To a guilty Imogen it sounded more like slave labour. 'No, it doesn't. I'll pay you the same money Mr Harding gets,' she said firmly, secretly flooded with contrition. 'Now, how do you like your coffee, Gabriel?'

CHAPTER TWO

ONE disadvantage of living alone in a newly restored house like Beech Cottage was how little effort it took to keep it immaculate. By mid-morning Imogen could rarely think of anything more to do in her home. Not that Beech Cottage felt like a permanent home. But now that the house in town was sold the cottage was all the home she had.

The builders were due back in two weeks to finish the boundary walls at the back of the garden and restore the summer house. Then Beech Cottage could be advertised in glowing estate-agent-speak, and she would retreat to London to a flat in the heart of the capital, with theatres, shops and restaurants on her doorstep, and she would look for a job so that time would never hang heavy again. She was a highly qualified, experienced PA who had worked for Philip Lambert for years before she finally became his wife.

Philip had been vice-chairman of an international bank. He had expected his personal assistant to cope with VIPs, heads of state, Members of Parliament as well as the actual nitty-gritty of coping with correspondence. He had demanded someone expert not only in the latest computer technology but in verbatim shorthand that she could transcribe into polished prose with faultless syntax.

Imogen stood at the ironing-board in the kitchen, her expression absent as she remembered the buzz and

21

excitement of organising complex travel arrangements, seminars, banquets—even golf days, and any other form of entertainment Philip's clients had required. She returned to her ironing, her lips compressed at the memory of the day when Philip told her that he was going to retire. She'd been his wife for two years by that time. When he'd retired she'd had no choice but to do the same. But she'd done so willingly, because she'd loved him and what he'd wanted she'd done her best to want just as much.

She came out of her reverie with a start as the one o'clock news began on the radio. Imogen frowned. What was Gabriel doing about lunch? She hadn't thought to ask him where he lived, but a large motorcycle was parked alongside the garage so he obviously lived some distance away.

She unplugged the iron and went out into the garden. He was nowhere to be seen, but the motorcycle was still there. She hesitated, then went along to the garden shed, where she found him sprawled in the rickety deckchair, eating sandwiches from an open container on the floor beside him. His eyes were closed and his earphones in place as usual as he finished the last of his lunch. Wishing there were some other way of attracting his attention, Imogen put a finger lightly on his warm, bare arm. He opened his eyes, switched off his radio and came to his feet in one spare, graceful movement.

'Sorry, Mrs Lambert, I didn't see you.'

What did he listen to? Pop music, classics? Whatever it was he seemed addicted to it. He was never without the earphones unless actually talking to her.

'I wondered if you'd like some coffee or tea. I forgot to ask if you lived locally—whether you'd be going home for lunch,' she said lightly.

'I do live locally, but I'd rather stay here for a short lunch-break and get on with the job,' he said, joining her outside in the sunshine. 'I'll leave at four, if that's all right with you. Six and a half hours.'

'Seven,' contradicted Imogen. 'I won't dock your lunch-break.'

'Thank you.'

'Do you prefer payment each day, or at the end of the week?'

To her surprise he looked disconcerted. He shrugged. 'You can pay me when I leave, after the job's finished.'

'Are you sure that's satisfactory?' Odd, she thought. She'd have thought a man like Gabriel would want some of his wages to spend at the weekend.

'Perfectly, Mrs Lambert.' He smiled. 'And the coffee you mentioned would be very welcome.'

She went back to the house to fill the coffee-machine. While she waited for it to perform she made herself a sandwich from the ham bought the day before, and pondered without enthusiasm on what to have for dinner. Salad again, probably, because she'd forgotten to buy any other vegetables. Not that it mattered. She had only herself to please. Almost her sole pleasure in living alone was not having to bother to cook.

When she went back into the garden Gabriel had vacated the shed and was tackling another border. She watched him wield the secateurs, admiring his expertise for a moment before he caught sight of her and got to his feet, thanking her as he took the outsize mug.

'In this heat I thought you could do with some extra liquid intake,' she said lightly.

'Thank you.' He waved a hand towards the wild area behind the laurels bordering the lawn at the back of the house. 'Ever thought of a vegetable garden back there, Mrs Lambert?'

She pulled a face. 'Absolutely not! The garden daunts me enough now. As is embarrassingly obvious by the state of the place, gardening is something new in my life.'

'Are you fond of vegetables?' he asked, draining the mug.

'Very. I was just scolding myself for forgetting to buy any when I went into the village yesterday.'

'I could go and fetch some for you after I finish,' he offered.

'That's very kind,' she said coolly, taking the mug from him, 'but I wouldn't dream of troubling you. I've got plenty of salad things. I'll make do with those tonight and take a walk into the village tomorrow.'

He inclined his head in grave acknowledgement not only of her decision, she noted, but of her abrupt retreat into lady-of-the-house mode. Which was wiser than being over-friendly. She had even decided against asking his first name. It wouldn't do for Gabriel to think that she had any Lady Chatterley tendencies. All she wanted from him, attractive young male though he was, was his labour in her garden.

She took him tea and biscuits at three, and at four he knocked at the open kitchen door to tell her that he'd finished for the day.

'Thank you,' she said briskly. 'You've done a lot in just one day.'

'Not as much as I hoped.' He smiled wryly. 'It's a long time since any real weeding was done here, Mrs Lambert. Some of the root systems go a long way. But once I've cleared everything properly you'll be able to cope more easily, even if you can't find a gardener on a regular basis.'

'I'm grateful,' she responded with what she hoped was the right blend of reserve and enthusiasm, and forbore to mention that the moment the time was right Beech Cottage would be put up for sale. The new owners, not she, would reap the benefits of his labours.

She stood at the kitchen window, listening to the roar of the motorbike recede down the lane, and suddenly loneliness washed over her in a wave. She'd exchanged a few words three times during the day with Gabriel, which hardly constituted enjoying his company, yet now that he'd gone the house seemed empty. Which was silly. The furthest he'd set foot in it was a yard into the kitchen.

She went upstairs to find something to occupy herself. She'd washed a couple of pairs of jeans, some bits of underwear and three T-shirts, as requested by Tash, but she'd forgotten about the passport.

Tash lacked Imogen's passion for order. The drawers in the cream-painted dresser were a jumble of discarded clothes which Imogen folded neatly into separate piles, but there was no passport. The set of dark carved pine shelves standing on the chest held lurid paperbacks and weightier English classics, an inverted horseshoe, photographs in frames, a wicker bowl of earrings—most of them odd. Imogen eyed them, smiling indulgently. Tash was pretty, clever, energetic and loving, but chronically untidy. The room owed its present air of order to her month-long absence.

It was a pleasing, welcoming room, decorated in deference to Tash's eclectic taste. The wicker rocking-chair was piled with cushions and the walls were plain cream paint with a deep, bold frieze of ivy leaves and berries which matched the curtains, tied back with cream silk ropes. The willow fence panel, which served as headboard, was an idea copied from a magazine, and piled pillows in stiff white linen covers, edged with handmade lace, lay against a honey-coloured quilt, all donated by Grandma Barbara.

There was no dressing-table as such, only an oval mirror with a carved pine frame over a shelf holding the few toiletries that Tash had left at the cottage. But a cuddly lion with a chewed mane lay on the quilt. Imogen unzipped the pyjama case and hauled out a T-shirt that Tash had worn to bed during her last visit, a volume of Shakespeare's sonnets—and the passport. She seized it, but her smile of triumph faded as a small snapshot fluttered loose. A lump in her throat, she stared at a younger, smiling Philip, with a baby Natasha in the crook of one arm, the other round a slender, smiling blonde girl—Louise, Natasha's mother.

Imogen put the snapshot back in the pyjama case and took the passport into her own room to put away in safety. Then she took the T-shirt downstairs and washed it out in the kitchen sink, afterwards hanging it out to dry in the warm evening sunshine.

As she returned to the house she heard the roar of a motorcycle along the lane, and to her astonishment a familiar figure leapt off the machine at the gate and took off the disguising helmet. Gabriel came striding up the path towards her, his dark-lashed eyes filled with silvery light in the sunshine as he held out a carrier bag.

'Hello again, Mrs Lambert. I thought you might like some vegetables for your dinner after all.'

Imogen, blue-devilled until a few minutes before, gave him a radiant smile. 'You went shopping for me? That's so kind of you, Gabriel—how much do I owe you?'

He shook his head. 'These are from the garden. We've a glut of broad beans at the moment. I hope you like them.'

She felt deeply touched. 'Why, thank you. I do.'

'Just cook them in salted water for a few minutes. Good with crisp grilled bacon and a few potatoes,' he said to her surprise. 'Simple, but a favourite summer supper of mine.'

'Do you include cooking in your talents?' she asked teasingly, and he shrugged.

'When necessary. I'm no chef, but I don't starve when left to fend for myself.'

She looked at him for a moment, then said on impulse, 'Would you like a drink, Gabriel, or is someone waiting for you?'

'Yes to the first,' he said promptly, 'and no to the second.'

She led the way into the house, and found that his carrier bag contained not only beans but slim new carrots, small potatoes and a head of freshly picked lettuce. 'All this looks so delicious. My compliments on your gardening, Gabriel.'

'My mother's the one with green fingers,' he said quickly. 'I just supply the muscles now and then.'

And very impressive muscles they were, she couldn't help thinking as she put the vegetables away. 'What can I give you? Whisky? Wine? Beer?'

Gabriel chose a glass of beer, and waited until she was sitting opposite him at the table before accepting her invitation to sit down.

'How do you like it here at Abbots Munden?' he asked, and she smiled wryly.

'In my particular circumstances—which you already know—it's a little difficult to settle in very well. The village is so attractive that it seems rude not to say I love it here, but to be honest I feel very much the outsider. I only recently came to live here permanently. Up until two months ago I only came down on the odd weekend, or if the builder wanted to see me.'

He drank some of the beer, looking thoughtful, and very, very attractive by any standards, she thought. What did a young man like him do for entertainment in a place like this? His company must surely be much sought after. Or perhaps he was married, and liked nothing better than going home to his wife every night after a hard day's work. Yet he'd said that he had no one waiting.

Tonight he was wearing a thin white cotton shirt with a rather more respectable pair of jeans than previously, his bare feet in white-soled canvas deck shoes, and after his day in the sun his tan was more pronounced than ever. His presence was a vital, living thing in the room, so much so that to her horror she felt a leap of physical response to it.

'I think people are probably reluctant to intrude on your grief,' he said at last.

'Yes, I rather thought that was the case,' said Imogen, knowing that she sounded cool in her pains to keep the employer-employee distinction plain between them. 'I'm not complaining, Gabriel. Everyone's been courtesy itself. But in the circumstances I find it hard to think of Beech Cottage as home. I'm town-born and bred. I've never lived in the country before.'

He smiled. 'I rather gathered that. Do you miss the pace of city life?'

'I'm afraid I do.' She shrugged. 'Though in this weather there's a lot to be said for the country. A lot of people would change places with me.' Her face shadowed. 'Where I live, I mean.'

'But you're lonely,' he said quietly. 'No family?'

'Parents dead, one brother in New Zealand, a couple of elderly uncles in Norfolk.' She smiled briskly. 'Another beer?'

Taking this for the dismissal it so very plainly was, he rose to his feet. 'No, thanks, Mrs Lambert. Time I was off.'

'Thank you again for the vegetables—and the suggested menu,' she added with a warmer smile. 'I'll try it out this very evening.'

He gave her no answering smile in response. 'Tell me to mind my own business, Mrs Lambert, but I think you ought to get out more, see more people, have friends to stay. Life has to go on.'

She stiffened. 'I'm sure you're right,' she said frostily. 'Goodnight, Gabriel.'

When he'd gone she hesitated, on the point of making herself yet another sandwich, then with a shrug she began scrubbing some of the tiny potatoes he'd brought her, shelled some of the beans and put the grill on to cook the bacon.

And when the meal was ready, instead of taking it on a tray into the sitting-room, Imogen sat on one of the spindle-back chairs at the oak dining-table set for one, with her good china and a Waterford crystal glass for her mineral water. Instead of hardly noticing what she ate while she read a book, she listened to some Delius while she enjoyed the meal, which, just as Gabriel had said, was simple and delicious, and more to her taste than anything she'd eaten in a long time.

She gave up trying not to think about him during the meal. He was something of an enigma. A gardener he might be, but his voice and vocabulary literally spoke of a good education, hinting at a background similar to Philip's. Perhaps Gabriel was a horticulturalist by profession, did landscape gardening or wrote books about it, young as he was. His tan was so deep-dyed that it had to come from long hours spent outdoors.

But some things about him didn't fit somehow. The Harley-Davidson motorcycle, the speakers clamped permanently in his ears, the overlong hair—these were the adjuncts of the youthful male. Yet in some ways he was not as youthful as she'd first thought—though he was a lot younger than herself. He exuded health and energy and vitality in a way only possible in youth. Which was undeniably appealing to a woman who'd been married to a man twenty-five years older than herself.

Her musings came skidding to a halt. She jumped to her feet to clear away, angry with herself. Philip had been just as energetic and vital in his own way. She washed up in a hurry, as though the hot water and suds would cleanse even the hint of mental infidelity from her mind, and, when she'd finished, she made herself a pot of extra-strong coffee and took it with a book into the room she'd put together with such careful understatement.

The biscuit and white stripes of the covers on the chairs and sofa blended well with the muted gold tint of the walls. A jewel-like Persian rug glowed in the centre of the pale fringed carpet, which was laid to leave a two-foot border of glowing, polished wood floor. A triple mirror with a gold Venetian frame topped the stone fireplace, where she had arranged tall spikes of creamy yellow lupins and shiny green mahonia leaves in the basket that she used for logs in the winter. The room was a success, both cool and warmly welcoming. Its only flaw was the lack of company to share it.

Next morning Imogen was up early after a night as restless and disturbed as most of her nights were now that she was alone. The sun was shining in a deep blue sky outside, the birds were singing and she felt both tired and restless as she ate her usual slice of wholemeal toast and drank cup after cup of strong, sugarless coffee. Yet underneath it all she felt a half-ashamed frisson of anticipation, because young Gabriel would shortly be here.

She shook her head in sudden distaste. She'd never understood how women could enjoy the company of men much younger than themselves, had looked down her nose at the idea. Yet now, at thirty-two years old, she was excited at the prospect of seeing a man more in her stepdaughter's age-range than her own. She grimaced at the thought, picturing Tash's face if she were ever to see Imogen's new gardener in the flesh.

Gabriel arrived as the clock in the hall struck nine. She heard the roar of the motorcycle and ran to the window, then dodged back as he bounded up the path to the kitchen door, which she'd purposely left open. By the time he reached it she was sitting, serene, at the kitchen table, the daily paper propped against the marmalade jar as though she'd just finished breakfast, instead of having eaten it nearly two hours before.

'Good morning, Gabriel,' she said brightly. 'Another lovely day.'

'Wonderful, Mrs Lambert.' He smiled at her, looking fit and rested and full of vitality. 'Anything in particular you'd like me to do first today? Or shall I get on with the borders?'

'Fine. I leave it all in your obviously capable hands,' she said, returning the smile. 'By the way, your menu was inspired. I loved the beans.'

'Did you do them with bacon?' he said, looking pleased.

She nodded. 'And your potatoes. Nicest meal I've had in a long time.'

'Good. I only wish that the asparagus hadn't finished. You'd have enjoyed that too.'

'I'm not too keen on asparagus.'

'You'd have liked mine,' he said with certainty, and took himself off to collect some tools from the garden shed.

He was probably right, she conceded as she began some unnecessary housework. No doubt everything he grew was as delicious as—as he was? Startled, she began cleaning windows, a task she'd never performed herself before coming to Beech Cottage. She turned the radio up loud and rubbed and polished until every window on the ground floor was gleaming and she was hot and untidy and her energies expended in more respectable ways than lingering on Gabriel's charms.

When she took coffee to him mid-morning a lot of questions clamoured in her mind at the sight of him. Did he have a wife or a girlfriend? Did he have some other job to return to after the two weeks he'd promised to spare her? What did he do for entertainment in this quiet, remote village?

'Tell me, Gabriel,' she said, when he'd thanked her for the coffee, 'what do you listen to on those headphones of yours?'

'Trollope,' he said succinctly.

She eyed him suspiciously. Was 'Trollope' some obscure, head-banging rock group?

'Anthony Trollope,' he went on, grinning from ear to ear. '*Barchester Towers* on tape. I enjoy having someone read to me while I work.'

She stared at him, taken aback, then started to laugh, and explained why.

'Tut-tut, Mrs Lambert,' he said reprovingly. 'We toilers in the earth have brains just like anyone else, you know.'

'I apologise,' she said, with not altogether joking contrition. 'But loud rock music just seemed to go with the image—the motorcycle and so on.'

'Borrowed plumes,' he said, amused. 'The bike is the pride of my young brother's life, but I paid for some repairs so he's kindly consented to let me use it while he's away. He's digging too, only instead of vegetables he hopes to turn up some archaeological find on the site of a Roman villa excavation in Norfolk.'

'Oh, I see.' Which wasn't exactly true. Imogen's picture of Gabriel and his family background was getting more out of focus by the minute. 'Would you like some more coffee?' she asked rather awkwardly.

'I would very much, only you needn't wait on me. I'll come and fetch it.'

As they walked back to the house together she became steadily more conscious of his proximity, of the scent of his warm skin and the faint, lemony aroma of something he'd used that morning.

'Do you ever listen to books on tape?' he asked, leaning in the kitchen doorway as she refilled his mug.

'No—I'd never thought of it.' She shrugged. 'I just read in the usual way.'

'Do you have trouble sleeping?' he asked bluntly. 'Your eyes are very beautiful, but there are dark marks below them.'

The compliment neatly deprived her of speech. To cover the fact she busied herself with pouring more coffee that she didn't want, then nodded casually. 'Only to be expected under the circumstances,' she said in a way intended to remind him exactly what those circumstances were.

'But you don't take sleeping pills?'

'No, I did at—at the time. But it didn't seem wise to make it a habit.'

'Well, listening to someone read a book on tape is a great way to get to sleep.' He smiled a little. 'I usually have to rewind the tape to find my place next day. I tend to nod off mid-sentence.'

Imogen's eyes lit up. 'In that case I'm eager to try. Where do I get some? Bookshops?'

'Yes. Or you can borrow them from the local library.' He hesitated. 'But you needn't do that to start with. I've got several. My mother has too. You can borrow what you like, see how you get on.'

This should be interesting, she thought. Now I get to know his mother's taste in literature as well as Gabriel's. 'Thank you,' she said sincerely. 'Perhaps you'd bring me one tomorrow?'

'With pleasure—I won't walk across your floor in these boots,' he added, and held out his empty mug. 'Thank you. I was thirsty.' As she took the mug from him he raised a questioning eyebrow. 'What kind of fiction do you like?'

She shrugged. 'Gory thrillers, historical novels— most things really, except science fiction or any other kind of fantasy.'

'I'll see what I can find at home,' he promised, and went back across the lawn to a herbaceous border which was already looking a great deal better for his attentions.

She washed the mugs, then collected ingredients for some walnut biscuits that Tash was fond of. She liked baking, but on her own rarely found the impetus to make things for herself. With Tash as an excuse she made a fruit cake as well as the biscuits, and rounded it off with a pie made from apples from the village shop teamed with raspberries from canes in the garden.

Having occupied herself until lunchtime, she provided Gabriel with coffee and a few of the biscuits to augment his sandwiches, then handed him a key.

'This is to the kitchen door,' she told him, 'so you can make yourself a drink this afternoon. I'm going into Cheltenham. Is there anything I should be buying for the garden?'

'You could do with some fertiliser and some organic slug pellets,' he told her, eyeing the key. 'But there's no need to give me this. I can survive until four, Mrs Lambert.'

'As you wish,' said Imogen, feeling faintly rebuffed, and went back into the house to shower. Afterwards she put on a slim cream linen skirt and a cream-striped beige silk sweater, fastening the heavy gold chain bracelet that Philip had given her to the wrist on which she already wore an oblong gold watch with a crocodile strap. She made up her face with more emphasis than usual, brushed her hair into a smooth topknot secured with gold pins, clipped chunky gold earrings to her lobes, put on her sunglasses and tucked her wallet into a small beige kid bag. She locked up and went past Gabriel on her way to the garage.

'I'll see you tomorrow, then, but tell me exactly what to get first,' she said briskly, aware that his eyes were appreciative as he took in her appearance. She wrote down the brand names he asked for in a small notebook, smiled her lady-of-the-house smile and went to get the car out, filled with the urge for noise and traffic and shops.

Suddenly she was desperate to get away from the house, the garden—and Gabriel. The reasons for escaping the first two were plain enough. Where Gabriel was concerned her reason was unclear. Nor did she intend any in-depth self-analysis on the subject, she thought acidly as she set off for the main road like a child let out of school.

CHAPTER THREE

IT WAS early evening by the time Imogen returned to the cottage. As she carried her packages into the house the air was so fragrant with the scent of roses and newly turned earth that it would have made her sad and restless if she hadn't been so tired.

Nothing like shopping to wear one out, she thought drily as she dumped her purchases on the kitchen table. As well as the unexciting things for the garden she'd bought food from a supermarket and delicacies from a department store's food hall.

Otherwise she'd just intended to do a little window-shopping, but in the end she'd succumbed to the temptation of a brief shift dress in a glorious shade of burnt orange that did wonders for her tan. She'd compounded the crime by adding a pair of fawn linen trousers and a silk waistcoat in a Paisley print of brown and cream and citrus yellow to wear over a filmy beige muslin shirt, then had cast caution aside completely and bought two identical pairs of low-heeled kid sandals, one in orange to match her dress, the other in an equally impractical citrus yellow.

She looked at the pile of carrier bags on the table and blew out her cheeks in dismay at her own extravagance. Where did she imagine that she was going to wear all this stuff? she asked herself. A couple of days of sunshine and she'd gone mad.

She hauled her loot up to her bedroom, then stood, arrested, as she caught sight of herself in the mirror. The other reason for her late return home was an hour spent with the hairdresser who'd agreed to fit her in without an appointment. He'd taken his time over trimming a few inches off her hair so that it tapered from a fringe across her forehead down into a glossy bob which swung inwards just below chin level, and altered her appearance not a little.

Philip had liked her hair long. But he's no longer here, she thought with sudden passion. And I am. And I've got to get a life again. A life of my own.

She took a swift shower, with the new haircut carefully protected in a towel, then on impulse put on the new trousers and the filmy shirt, added the waistcoat and the yellow sandals and took a long look at herself in the Victorian cheval-glass in the corner of the room. Philip, she thought, would hardly have recognised her. In the months of her widowhood she'd lost weight and gained a haunted look, which the new haircut went a long way to dispel. Maybe it was her own fancy, she thought, twisting this way and that to view her reflection, but she looked younger with shorter hair, less—less careworn.

The doorbell interrupted her preening. Her heart missed a beat and she forced herself to walk slowly as she went down the flight of uncovered, creaking wood stairs and crossed the hall to the kitchen, knowing before she opened the door who would be standing there.

'Hello, Gabriel,' she said, with commendable calm.

He said nothing for a moment. His eyes shuttered abruptly as they took in the clothes and the hair and the flushed face bare of make-up. He looked as though he too had just come from a shower. His curling hair was still damp and he was newly shaved, she noted, just as he'd been this morning. Not a devotee of designer stubble, obviously, though he was dark enough to make it an effort not to be. He wore khaki cotton trousers, a pale blue shirt and a pair of well-worn, polished brown loafers, and Imogen fought down a burning, dismaying gush of response as she looked at him.

'I hope I didn't disturb you, Mrs Lambert,' he said at last, his voice carefully neutral. He held out a carrier bag, just as he'd done the night before. 'No beans this time. I thought you might like a few of the tapes I mentioned.'

'How very kind.' Afraid to take the bag from him because her hands were trembling, she beckoned him inside. 'Do come in—can I get you a beer?'

'Thank you.' He put the bag on the table, accepted a frosty can and a glass, watching as she examined the tapes.

'*Northanger Abbey*!' she exclaimed, in command of herself again. She looked up with a smile. 'I haven't read any Jane Austen since I was in school.'

'Other than *Barchester Towers*—which you can have when I've finished them—the immortal Jane was the nearest thing to a historical novel I could find. Except that she was contemporary to the time she wrote about, of course.' He smiled. 'She's my mother's favourite.'

So his mother read Jane Austen as well as growing vegetables, she thought as she thanked him for two thrillers read by well-known actors. 'I'm a great fan of both authors, but I've missed these particular titles somewhere.' She looked up. 'It was very thoughtful of you to come back this evening, Gabriel. I appreciate it.'

He met the look steadily. 'I didn't like to think of you lying awake in the night.' He paused. 'You *do* have a radio with a tape deck?'

'Yes, I do.' She laughed. 'Why? Were you going to provide me with that as well?'

'If necessary,' he agreed, grinning. 'Did you enjoy the trip to Cheltenham?'

'Actually I did, very much. I haven't left the village much lately, which is just as well after my extravagance today.' She waved a hand at her clothes. 'I went on rather a wild shopping spree. All this is new. And I had my hair cut too.' Why am I telling him all this? she thought in sudden embarrassment.

'It looks wonderful,' he assured her. 'I like the clothes too.' Then, as if suddenly mindful of the boundary between them, Gabriel finished the beer and stood up. 'I must be going, Mrs Lambert. I hope you enjoy the books.'

'I'm sure I will.' She went with him to the door. 'Thank your mother for Jane Austen.'

He nodded. 'I will. Goodnight.'

It was becoming a habit to listen to the roar of the Harley-Davidson as Gabriel departed. Imogen sighed. Such a pity that she couldn't have asked him to stay to supper. But perhaps it was just as well. Her physical reaction to him was something to clamp down on before it got out of hand. Yet quite apart from his considerable physical attraction she liked him more and more as she got to know him. He was remarkably kind, too. Few young men of his age would have taken the trouble to come back in their free time, first with vegetables, now with audio books to help her to get to sleep.

Northanger Abbey, which she had once read with bored reluctance, proved so entertaining when read by Anna Massey that the cure for sleep was not as immediate as Gabriel had predicted. Imogen was on side three, and it was well into the small hours, before she slept. She woke the next morning a lot later than usual, but with a smile for the first time in many long months as she realised that Gabriel had been right about having to rewind the tape to get back to the part she remembered. His cure for insomnia had been very effective.

When he arrived, punctual as usual, she told him as much as she gave him a cup of coffee from the pot she was only halfway through after her late start. Some of the lateness was due to her taking the trouble to shower and choose something rather more appealing than her usual jeans, she knew very well, but the effort had been worth it. Gabriel's eyes told her plainly that she was easy to look at in a pink-striped white shirt knotted over a white camisole and raspberry-red linen trousers. Her tan had decided her to dispense with make-up altogether, and that the effect was pleasing was something he made no attempt to hide.

'You look very well this morning, Mrs Lambert,' he commented. 'Did the tapes work?'

'They certainly did. I got rather involved with Jane Austen, but then I fell asleep halfway through the third side, just as you said.' She smiled. 'It was almost two before that happened, but then I slept like a log until half an hour ago. Which was sheer bliss.'

'I'm glad,' he said simply, and put the cup down. 'I'd better get on before the sun gets too hot.'

'If it does, just stop,' she said firmly. 'Don't get sunstroke over a few weeds.'

'I've brought a hat today.' He grinned. 'An old cricket hat of Hector's—my brother. Mine was too disreputable.'

'You like cricket?'

'Both of us play for the village team when we can. There's a match on Sunday. Why not come? Hector can't make it, of course, but I've promised Tom Jennings I'll open against Long Hinton.'

'Open?' said Imogen.

'Bat first—take the edge off the bowling.' He grinned. 'Ted Berridge, landlord of the Drover's Arms in Long Hinton, fancies himself as a demon bowler.'

'Sounds exciting—I may come at that,' she said lightly, privately thinking it very unlikely. Unlike many women she liked cricket, but wasn't sure she could brave turning up alone at the Abbots Munden cricket pitch.

The week seemed to have gone by surprisingly quickly. Time seemed to hang less heavily with Gabriel around during the day, and the prospect of Tash's company on the Saturday gave an added spice to life. Then, on Friday afternoon, Tash rang up, her voice full of contrition, to say that Saturday was difficult, so could she make it Sunday instead and stay over until Monday.

'I hope this doesn't spoil your plans, Imogen,' said Tash anxiously. 'Will the fatted calf keep a day?'

'Of course,' she said, pleased to hear that Tash would be staying the night.

'Thanks, you're an angel. I'll be there in time for lunch. Someone's giving me a lift.'

Imogen was unsurprised. Tash hadn't learnt to drive as yet but seemed in no hurry to master the art because, as she'd explained so cheerfully, one of her string of friends, male and female, always seemed ready to ferry her wherever she wanted to go.

When Imogen took Gabriel his afternoon drink she told her that he'd like to come back for just an hour or two the following morning, if she was agreeable.

'I can't finish this hedge this afternoon,' he said, putting down the powered hedge-cutter which he'd brought along that morning. 'And it'll look pretty odd if I leave it half done. I need to prune in places before I can use the machine, which makes it pretty slow work. It's a long time since anyone did a thorough job on this lot.'

'Won't it wait until Monday?' she asked.

'The weather might break. I'd like to finish it.' He hesitated. 'I could work later tonight instead, if you prefer.'

'Up to you entirely.' She smiled. 'I can always rise to some overtime, if that's any help.'

He stiffened, his face darkening. 'Certainly not. I didn't mean that, Mrs Lambert.'

'Sorry, sorry,' she said hastily. 'Anyway, your choice, Gabriel. Tonight or tomorrow—it makes no difference to me.'

'Then I'll stay later today.' He turned away, picked up the hedge-cutter and yanked it into life, putting an effective end to the conversation. She went back to the house, pulling a face. She'd offended him with the mention of extra money. Touchy young man— she'd tread more warily in future.

It was six-thirty before he finished to his satisfaction, which meant that Imogen had to go without the session of sunbathing that she indulged in every day once he'd gone roaring off down the lane. It was impossible to stretch out on the terrace in shorts and a vest-top, in full view as he worked.

To fill in the time she made a ham and egg pie to go with the chicken that she intended to roast to eat cold on Sunday when her stepdaughter came. Natasha Lambert had an appetite like a construction worker's, and was fortunate that her rounded curves weren't a lot more rounded than they were, considering the food she packed away.

Cooking was something that Imogen had never had much time for during her working life. Philip had liked to take her out to eat, and when they had eaten at home had preferred steaks and salads and pasta dishes rather than a conventional roast. But since her permanent residence at Beech Cottage her culinary horizons had widened. Pastry was a new accomplishment, as was the concoction of various dressings and sauces. There'd been no time for such things once. Now there was far too much.

Gabriel came to the door at six-thirty, sweating and dusty, weariness replacing his usual boundless vitality for once. 'Right, Mrs Lambert, I'm off home now.'

'Wouldn't you like a beer first before you go?' she asked quickly, sure that he must be dehydrated after all his efforts.

'No, thanks,' he said, unsmiling. 'I'm too dirty.'

So she was still unforgiven. 'Look, Gabriel,' she said bluntly, 'if I offended you with the offer of extra money, I'm sorry. But I don't expect anyone to work for me for nothing. Today you've been here nine and a half hours, which is what you'll be paid for when we settle up. It's not overtime—just wages due to you.'

For a moment she thought that he was going to tell her just what she could do with her money, then his face relaxed. 'Thank you. The apologies should be mine. But I didn't want you to think I was cadging extra hours.'

She shook her head. 'Maybe I'm just an ignorant outsider unused to country ways, but surely it's not a hanging offence to discuss overtime, Gabriel? I thought the labourer was worthy of his hire.'

He thrust his sweat-soaked hair back from his forehead, a strange expression in his eyes. 'You're right of course. But I haven't worked for a—a lady before.'

She laughed. 'Then in future you'll just have to pretend I'm a man and you won't feel embarrassed.'

'Mrs Lambert, it would be impossible to regard a beautiful woman like you as a man.' His eyes gleamed as he saw her colour rise, and suddenly he didn't look in the least tired. He gave her a little salute, said goodnight and turned away before she could think of anything to say. Then halfway down the path he turned, cajolery in the smile he gave her. 'Shall I see you on Sunday at the match?'

'Afraid not—I've got someone coming.'

The smile vanished. 'I see. Right, I'll be back on Monday, then. Goodnight.'

'Goodnight—and good luck with the cricket.'

After a day spent entirely alone, free to sunbathe as much as she liked, Imogen was glad when Saturday was over and the arrival of Tash imminent on Sunday morning. She had a cold lunch ready, the defrosted raspberry and apple pie warming gently in the oven, and had arrayed herself in the new orange dress, when there was a squeal of brakes, a slamming of car doors, and Natasha Lambert came running up the path to the kitchen door, a large young man loaded with luggage following at a slower rate behind her.

She threw herself into Imogen's arms, hugged her and kissed her on both cheeks, then stood back and gave a raucous, vulgar whistle. 'Wow, you look fan-tastic! I *love* the hair, and that colour's amazing on you—oh, by the way, this is Nat Soames. He's on the same floor in hall. Nat, this is my wicked stepmother.'

The young man, apparently stunned at the sight of Imogen, said something incoherent by way of greeting, obligingly hefted Tash's bags up to her room, came downstairs to drink a quick cup of coffee, then was sped on his way by Tash. She waltzed with him to the gate, gave him a quick, impersonal hug, then waved him off in the Deux Chevaux and ran back to Imogen, her long, flaxen hair flying and her blue eyes bright as she explained there'd been a party the night before. Nat had coaxed her to go to it by promising to drive her here this morning.

'So you're not miffed with me, are you?'

'Of course not,' Imogen assured her. 'You've been to see Barbara and Henry, of course.'

'Of course! Since I'm in college in Egham and they live in Windsor I can hardly fail to, can I?' Tash grinned. 'Anyway, Grandma fills my biscuit tins with goodies while I play backgammon with Grandpa, so I'd be a fool to keep away, wouldn't I?'

'I hope you're suitably grateful,' said Imogen severely.

'Of course I am.' Tash sobered suddenly. 'I think the world of them. I don't go just for the pecan cookies!'

'I know you don't.' She eyed her stepdaughter's khaki shorts and grubby white T-shirt. 'If you take those off I'll wash them for you to take with you. What did you wear to the party last night?'

'These, of course,' gurgled Tash, stripping off un-selfconsciously in the middle of the kitchen floor. 'Thanks, love; I'll just dash upstairs and take a shower. What's for lunch?'

They ate their meal on the terrace under an umbrella, Tash lavish with her praise of Imogen's new talent with pastry. 'Gosh, this ham and egg thing's wonderful. More, please!'

It was only when the raspberry and apple pie had been eaten, along with a scoop of ice-cream on Tash's part, that she noticed the garden.

'I say, you have been working hard. It was getting distinctly junglified last time I was here.'

'Alas, I cannot tell a lie,' sighed Imogen. 'It's all the work of the man I found.'

'Oh, right, you did mention it.' Tash looked at the immaculate lawns and the weed-free herbaceous borders with respect. 'He must be good.'

'He is.' She hesitated. 'He's quite young, actually, to be so knowledgeable about gardening. He's only doing it on a temporary basis until I can get someone permanent.'

'Why? Has he got another job?'

'I don't know. He doesn't volunteer much about himself, and I don't like to bombard him with questions.' She looked away across the garden to the hedges that Gabriel had worked so hard to trim. 'He's rather reserved, but very kind. He brings me vegetables from his own place. That's his lettuce you've been eating.'

Tash eyed her thoughtfully. 'Exactly how young is he?'

Imogen shrugged. 'No idea. Older than you, but younger than me. If you want the details he's tall, with longish black hair, comes here on a Harley-Davidson, and works with earphones plugged in all day.'

'Head-banger?'

'No. He listens to taped novels on his Walkman. He's working his way through my garden while someone reads Trollope to him—Barchester Towers to be exact.'

'Wow!' Tash's blue eyes were like saucers. 'Will he be here tomorrow before I leave?'

'Oh, yes. Gabriel's very punctual. Arrives at nine on the dot.' Imogen grinned. 'Why? Have I whetted your curiosity?'

'Too right you have,' declared Tash. 'Gabriel what? Or is it his surname?'

Imogen had to confess that she had no idea.

Tash shook her head in disapproval. 'Honestly, Imogen, he's working for you and you don't even know his name? Tut-tut! Anyway, he's an angel if he's helped you out, whatever his name is. Does he look angelic?'

'Not in the least,' said Imogen firmly. 'Too dark.'

'Must all angels have golden hair, then?'

'Since I've never met one, I have no idea!'

Tash jumped up to take in the used plates. 'You stay here, Imogen. I'll see to these. Shall I put them in the dishwasher?'

'I never use it.' Imogen shrugged. 'Hardly worth it just for one.'

Tash put the plates back on the table and dropped down beside her, putting her arms round her and rubbing her warm, young cheek against the newly cut red-brown hair. 'Is it getting better, Imogen? When I saw you today I hoped you were on the mend.'

'I am,' she assured her, returning the hug. 'I can't see myself settling here permanently without your father, but I'm getting better at thinking of myself as a self-contained unit instead of one of a pair.'

'I miss him too,' said Tash huskily.

'I know, I know, darling. But he'd hate it if you moped. He'd want you to get on with your life.'

Tash raised her fair curly head and looked into her eyes. 'He'd want you to get on with yours too.'

'I will. Once this place is finished I'll put it on the market, buy a flat in town, and you can decorate your bedroom there any way you like.'

Tash sighed and got up. 'I like my room just the way it is here. But it wouldn't do in town. I just love the cottage. Do you have to sell? Couldn't you keep it as a weekend place? Or won't the funds allow?'

Imogen gazed at her stepdaughter in surprise. 'I suppose I could. If I get another job, as I intend to, I might just rise to a place in town and this one, I suppose.' She hesitated. 'I thought you might not want to stay here, darling. That you might miss your father too much.'

Tash shook her head firmly. 'I would have done in the London house. That was chock-full of Dad. But he's not here in this place at all—at least not for me.'

Left alone, Imogen thought over Tash's statement at some length. She'd had no idea that Tash adored Beech Cottage so much. And Imogen could see what she meant about Philip. He'd been a creature of city pavements who'd lived his life at a punishing pace. There was nothing of him here at all. She was lonely without him, of course. But she'd feel like that wherever she was, town or country. And with the garden looking so much better she realised for the first time that she'd be loath to leave Beech Cottage herself. Now.

Tash came back with a tray of coffee, and plumped herself down on the other chair at the table. 'Right, then, Stepmama, what shall we do the rest of the day—except talk our heads off? Sunbathe? Watch television? Or is there some rural form of entertainment on offer in Abbots Munden?'

'Actually,' said Imogen, with sudden inspiration, 'there is. How do you feel about village cricket?'

CHAPTER FOUR

TASH was surprisingly enthusiastic about watching the village team play, and promptly changed from frayed denim shorts and ancient vest into a long, sweeping flowered skirt, a white scooped-neck top and a waistcoat apparently knitted from string. Hessian sandals and hoop earrings completed the outfit.

'I wouldn't have thought that cricket was your cup of tea,' said Imogen as she collected her straw hat.

'Where there is cricket there are men,' said Tash with relish. 'There's something so erotic about lots of suntanned men in elegant white disporting themselves on the green sward and all that.'

'I hope lots of women are there too,' returned Imogen with misgiving. 'We'd be a touch conspicuous as the only female Abbots Munden supporters.'

She needn't have worried. When they reached the field behind the church a surprisingly large number of enthusiasts of both sexes were crowded near the old green pavilion, and when they arrived Tom Jennings was busily deploying his team to key fielding positions as Len Baldwin, who ran the local minicab service, came on to deliver his tricky leg-spins to daunt the Long Hinton batting.

Before she had a chance to wonder where they'd sit, and what on, a young man in cricket whites came dashing up to them with a pair of folding canvas chairs.

'Mrs Lambert?' he queried, suddenly beetroot-red as he came face to face with Tash.

'Yes. How kind. Are those for us?' said Imogen warmly.

The youth nodded, swallowing. 'Gabriel told me to bring them. Where would you like to sit?'

'Where do you recommend?' said Tash, giving him a smile that shook him to the toes of his cricket boots.

'Under the t-trees here?' stammered the boy, getting into all sorts of trouble as he tried to unfold the chairs. 'You'll be in the shade—and n-not too near the boundary.'

'That's perfect,' said Imogen, wincing as he caught his finger in the second chair. 'Thank you so much. Are you from the village?'

He grinned shyly. 'No. I'm the enemy. I come in down the order a bit for Long Hinton.'

'Then it's very nice of you to take so much trouble with Abbots Munden supporters,' said Tash fervently.

'No trouble at all—my pleasure,' he assured her breathlessly. 'Must dash now. Time to pad up.'

'Cute boy,' observed Tash as they sat down in the chairs. 'By the way, where is the famous Gabriel?'

Imogen pretended to search the field for the man she'd spotted the moment they'd arrived. 'He's the dark one on the far boundary, running after the ball.'

Tash openly gaped as the graceful, lithe figure raced for the ball, picked it up, turned and shied it at the wicket all in one movement, the ball taking out the middle stump seconds before the panting batsman arrived at the crease. There was a great roar from players and watchers in unison as the panama-hatted umpire pointed a finger and sent the disconsolate batsman trudging back to the pavilion.

Tash turned to fix Imogen with incredulous blue eyes. 'Are you telling me that the hunk over there—the one putting his sunhat back on—is the man you found to weed the *garden*?'

'That's the one.'

'You never said he was gorgeous!'

'Is he?'

'Oh, come *on*, Imogen, you're not blind, neither was I born yesterday!' said Tash with spirit. 'You know perfectly *well* he's gorgeous.'

'He's good-looking, I suppose—'

'Good-looking? He's tall, and sexy and—wow, there he goes again. Look at the way he *moves*!'

'Quiet!' Imogen whispered fiercely, shrinking down in her chair. 'We're attracting enough attention just by turning up. So behave. I live here, remember.'

'Sorry,' said Tash, subsiding. 'Anyway,' she muttered, 'whatever you're paying him for the gardening it isn't enough!'

'Be quiet, you horrible child.'

Fortunately for Imogen the game began to get very exciting from then on. Len's leg spins at one end and Tom Jennings' accurate medium-pace bowling at the other proved too much for the next two batsmen, and suddenly the score was thirty for three.

'Oh, dear,' said Tash, clutching Imogen's arm. 'The gallant enemy's coming on next. I do hope he scores a run or two, poor lamb.'

Imogen nodded fervently, glad that Tash's attention was diverted from Gabriel. 'Not that I'm hopeful. He looks so frail, poor little lad.'

The 'poor little lad', however, proved to have an eye and hand in perfect concert, and sent the ball flashing over the boundary ropes twice for four before the sixth and final ball of the over was bowled.

'Gosh,' said Tash, impressed, as the field changed positions. 'He's good!'

'Left-hander too,' observed Imogen, who often watched test-match cricket on television. She relaxed, enjoying the sunshine and the game, not least because Gabriel was fielding too far away for Tash to demand an introduction.

From the roars of the visiting supporters they learned that the fragile-looking young Long Hinton batsman's name was Tony. He went on to score an impressive fifty before rashly swiping the ball skywards to the boundary, straight into the waiting hands of Gabriel.

'Dear me—bit of a star, your Gabriel,' muttered Tash, clapping vigorously as young Tony walked off the field.

'Star yes—mine no.'

'Do you wish he was?' came the swift reply.

'Don't be silly, Tash,' said Imogen, her voice sharper than she'd intended. 'Quite apart from his age—or lack of it—I'm hardly likely to get a crush on someone who works in my garden!' Somehow, in her rush to quash Tash's teasing, her reply had come out in a more pejorative way than she'd meant it to and she flushed as Tash accused her of snobbery.

'Certainly not,' she retorted, and stirred restlessly. 'Have you had enough? Shall we go home?'

But Tash, it seemed, was enjoying the afternoon hugely, and had no desire at all to go home. 'Imogen, please stay,' she begged. 'I'll stop being a pain and just sit here and enjoy the cricket.' Her face sobered. 'And it can't do you any harm, either, out here in the sunshine among other people, instead of alone at the cottage all the time. Dad wouldn't have wanted that.'

Defeated, Imogen sank back in her chair. 'I know he wouldn't. And of course we'll stay as long as you like.'

There was little opposition to the Abbots Munden bowling after Tony's innings; the visiting team were all out for one hundred and twenty just in time for the teams to take tea in the pavilion.

'I wish we could have tea too,' said Tash, sighing. 'I'm hungry.'

Imogen chuckled. 'How unusual—just say the word and we'll go home and have some.'

'Not on your life,' retorted Tash. 'We've got to cheer the home side on!'

Imogen made no protest, happy to look round her at the tree-edged field with the church spire beyond it, enjoying the peaceful, ineluctably English scene as she listened to Tash's account of the previous night's party.

'Are you sure you don't mind? That I'm going to France, I mean,' said Tash after a while.

'Not in the least,' said Imogen rather abstractedly, having spotted Gabriel wending his way towards them with a tray.

'I say,' whispered Tash in excitement, 'is he making for us?'

It quickly became obvious that not only was Gabriel coming towards them, but he intended providing them with tea.

'Good afternoon, Mrs Lambert,' he said as he reached them. 'Mrs Jennings sent me to say that she was very glad to see you here, and thought you might like some tea and cakes. She does the catering at these affairs.'

'Why, Gabriel, how—how very sweet of her,' said Imogen faintly, and managed a smile as he set the tray down on the grass. 'This is my daughter, Natasha.'

He straightened, staring blankly at Tash, who sprang from her chair, beaming, to shake his hand.

'Hi, Gabriel. Nice to meet you. Terrific catch just now.'

'How do you do?' He smiled belatedly. 'The ball seemed to hang in the air forever. I was shaking in my shoes, sure I'd drop the damn thing.'

Tash chuckled. 'If you say so. When do you go in to bat?'

'I open with Tom Jennings,' he said, and looked down at Imogen. 'I'm glad you came, Mrs Lambert.'

'So am I,' she returned serenely. 'It's been very entertaining so far. Thank you for arranging chairs for us, by the way. And for the tea,' she added. 'Please tell Mrs Jennings how much Tash and I appreciate it.'

'Especially me,' grinned Tash. 'I'm always hungry.'

Gabriel returned the grin, then glanced at his watch. 'I'd better get back to pad up. Enjoy your tea.'

'Good luck,' said Imogen, smiling. 'Will you beat Long Hinton, do you think?'

'We'll have a damn good try,' he assured her, and jogged away along the boundary line towards the pavilion.

'Golly,' said Tash in awe. 'What a chap! Ace cricketer, great looks, digs the garden, brings you tea. Archangel is right. Does he have a brother?'

'He does as it happens,' said Imogen sweetly. 'I believe his name's Hector. Now you be mother for once and pour the tea.'

Tash obeyed with alacrity, devouring one of Mrs Jennings' apricot muffins as she did so. 'Good move, coming here today,' she said indistinctly, then raised an accusing eyebrow at Imogen. 'By the way, what on earth possessed you to introduce me as your daughter?'

'Slip of the tongue,' she assured her. 'I rather tend to think of you as my daughter, anyway.'

'Oh.' Tash's eyes misted over for a moment. 'What a lovely thing to say.' She sniffed, and refilled Imogen's cup, and for a while there was silence as they finished their tea together.

'Shall I take the tray back?' asked Tash.

'If you would, darling. Thank Mrs Jennings for me.'

'Right.' Tash hefted the tray carefully, but had carried it only a yard or two before the eager young Long Hinton star batsman sprinted to relieve her of it. Imogen watched with amusement as Tony almost dropped his burden more than once as Tash chatted away to him in her usual friendly fashion. A few minutes later she ran back to her.

'Message delivered. They're just about to take the field. And Gabriel the Gorgeous is ready and waiting in pads and gloves, looking *very* impressive. I hope his batting matches his fielding.'

So do I, thought Imogen, shocked by how passionately she wanted him to do well. Her tension mounted as he sauntered down the pavilion steps, bat tucked under his arm, his face relaxed and smiling as he talked to Tom Jennings on the way to the wicket. But after the first over, during which Gabriel sent four of the six balls to the boundary, totting up sixteen runs, to the ecstasy of the home crowd, her tension vanished, never to return.

Tash howled with delight as she applauded, bouncing in her chair with an energy that threatened to collapse it. 'Does the England team know about Gabriel?' she demanded in excitement, and Imogen laughed.

'This is village cricket, not test-match stuff,' she reminded Tash. 'Though I must say he looks pretty useful with a bat.'

It soon became evident that Gabriel's opening partner, Tom Jennings, was a stonewall, defensive type of batsman, his role being to take the edge off the bowling. No runs were scored in the next over, then a hush fell over the spectators as Gabriel faced the demon bowler of Long Hinton, brought on early after the previous bowler's dismal failure.

The first two balls went hurtling down the wicket, to be played with a perfect forward stroke by Gabriel, but making no runs. The third ball was less accurate, and Gabriel punished it mercilessly, sending it sailing over the boundary for six. Imogen and Tash sat

forward, entranced, as the pattern of play for the
village team emerged. At one end batsman succeeded
batsman from time to time, each of them obviously
with only one aim—to stay in as long as possible while
Gabriel scored the runs.

When the church clock struck seven the game was
over, with four wickets in hand as Gabriel finished
off the game with a final boundary.

Tumultuous applause greeted his exit from the field.
Imogen and Tash stood up, joining in with enthusiasm as Gabriel waved his bat in acknowledgement and leapt up the steps to the pavilion,
looking as fresh as when he'd walked down them to
open the batting.

'Gosh, what a star!' said Tash with feeling as they
strolled home through the evening sunshine. 'Is he
really just a gardener, Imogen?'

'What's wrong with being a gardener?'

'Nothing at all. It's probably a wonderful, rewarding job for a lot of men. Sort of relaxing and
tranquil, artistic even. But Gabriel somehow doesn't
fit the part.'

Imogen laughed. 'What time are you leaving
tomorrow?'

'After lunch. Why?'

Gabriel reports for duty at nine in the morning. If
you're that curious, aim your questions at *him*.'

Tash was notoriously bad at getting up in the morning,
but next day she was up and dressed half an hour
before Gabriel was due. She joined Imogen at the
breakfast-table, looking rather sheepish.

'Good morning, darling,' said Imogen, raising a wry eyebrow. 'Couldn't you sleep?'

'Don't be sarcastic!' Tash grinned. 'I thought I'd be here when Gabe the Glorious arrived. Make it easier to saunter out and chat him up later, I thought.'

'Now don't go putting the poor boy through the third degree,' said Imogen severely. 'I don't want him frightened off. Bacon? Eggs? A sausage or two?'

'Yes, please.' Tash eyed her stepmother's elderly jeans and faded pink sweatshirt with disapproval. 'Haven't you anything more appealing to wear?'

Imogen shrugged. 'Don't worry—I'll change before Chris comes.'

'I was thinking more of Gabriel!'

She gave Tash a very direct look. 'These are the sort of clothes I wear in the mornings no matter who's around—Gabriel, the builder's men, even the vicar.'

Tash flushed bright red with remorse. 'I was only teasing, love.'

'I know. But enough, OK?'

'Right.' Tash took refuge behind the morning paper, reading bits of it to Imogen as the latter prepared her breakfast, so obviously contrite that Imogen relented as she set a plateful of sizzling food on the table. 'There. That should hold you for an hour or so.'

Tash nodded ecstatically and polished it off in record time, along with several pieces of toast, and half the fresh pot of coffee that Imogen made. When Gabriel appeared at the open kitchen door, wearing his usual uniform of ragged jeans and faded rugby shirt, Tash said nothing more than a friendly good morning, followed by warm congratulations on his performance.

'I hope you both enjoyed the match,' he said, after refusing Imogen's offer of coffee. 'I thought I might have talked to you afterwards, but you'd gone.'

Tash opened her mouth to say something, then thought better of it and shut it again as Imogen explained that she'd wanted to get home to put supper on.

'And thank you again for providing chairs, and bringing us tea,' she added with a smile. 'It was a very pleasant afternoon all round. Your innings was impressive.'

Gabriel shrugged. 'It was only village cricket, Mrs Lambert. But we all enjoy it. I try to turn out whenever I can.'

Tash was obviously dying to ask what prevented him from turning out for every match, but Imogen quelled her with a glance.

'Right, Gabriel, I hoped you might be able to do something with the wild patch at the back of the garden today,' she said briskly. 'Just some tidying up so it looks less like a wilderness.'

He nodded courteously and excused himself to make a start, leaving a rather pregnant silence behind him in the kitchen.

'You're very lady-of-the-manorish with him,' accused Tash.

'I don't mean to be.' Imogen flushed, knowing Tash was right. 'But it's just as well not to get too familiar with—'

'The hired help?'

'I meant with an attractive young man very much my junior who might misunderstand my motives and

run like hell if I got too friendly,' she said bluntly.
'And then *I'd* have to do the gardening.'

'You talk as though you were a hundred years old,'
said Tash scornfully. 'For pity's sake, Imogen, it's
time you joined the real world again. Dad's gone and
we both miss him like crazy, but you're still here, and
he'd want you to enjoy life.'

'What's that got to do with Gabriel?'

'It's just your attitude. Afraid to loosen up and
smile at the man in case he thinks you're about to
leap on him.'

'He's a boy, not a man—'

'You're a bit out there. All your talk about motor-
bikes and Walkmans had me expecting some callow
lad with more hormones than brains.' Tash eyed her
defiantly. 'Whereas Gabriel out there is a pretty
mature adult. And don't try and deny it.'

'Could we drop the subject?' said Imogen with
sudden impatience. 'Just hand over any washing left
hanging about and then you can go and tidy your
bedroom. I strongly object to the chaos up there every
time you descend on me.'

Tash stared at her with hurt blue eyes, then, without
a word, went out of the room and ran up the noisy,
creaking stairs, leaving Imogen appalled with herself
for snapping at her stepdaughter. What on earth was
the matter with her? She couldn't care less if Tash left
her room looking like a disaster area. There would be
time enough to tidy it up once she was on her way to
France.

Sighing, she waited half an hour then went upstairs
to tap on Tash's door. To her dismay she found her
stepdaughter sprawled face down on her bed in the

now immaculate room, her rounded young body still shaken by an occasional sob.

'Oh, Tash!' Aching with remorse, she pulled the girl up into her arms and held her close. 'Don't cry. I didn't mean to cut at you like that.'

'It's my fault for banging on about Gabriel and— and everything. Sorry I got on your nerves.' Tash sniffed, burrowing her head against Imogen.

They held each other close for comfort for a while, then Imogen put Tash away from her and smiled into her flushed face, her heart contracting at the girl's reddened eyelids. 'Not your fault that I'm so touchy. I'm sorry too,' she said remorsefully. 'I couldn't care less about the mess, really. What else do I have to do? Now, then, hand over your smalls and let's get them dry so you can pack.'

Mid-morning Imogen gave Natasha a cup of coffee and a slice of fruit cake to take to Gabriel. 'And don't hang about nattering to him for hours,' she warned. 'Gabriel's much too polite to tell you to get lost, and I pay him by the hour, remember.'

'Slave-driver! By the way,' Tash added guiltily, biting her lip, 'I asked Chris to lunch. Is that OK?'

Imogen gave her an exasperated smile. 'I can hardly say no, you monster. Why didn't you say so earlier?'

'Sorry—again!' Tash smiled winningly. 'There's lots of cold chicken and pie left over, and I'll make one of my special salads to save you any slaving over a hot stove in this weather. Which you might well have done.'

Which was the truth. Imogen ate alone so much that the prospect of company for a meal would have stampeded her into a roast that neither Tash nor Chris would have fancied before a long, hot drive.

Tash was back in a surprisingly short time with an empty mug and plate. 'He's nice, but not very talkative,' she reported, looking rather nettled. 'Though I must say he brightened a little when I mentioned that I'm your stepdaughter, *not* the actual fruit of your loins.'

'Dear heaven, I hope you didn't put it like that!' Imogen laughed helplessly, then set Tash to scraping potatoes to keep her occupied. Secretly she was pleased that Gabriel knew she wasn't the biological mother of a girl of eighteen. It was a good thing Tash had no idea that Gabriel occupied rather more of her stepmother's thoughts than was wise. Yet Tash, as was patently obvious from her attitude, would be only too happy if her father's widow took an interest in some man, which was surprising. Imogen had quite expected her to feel hostile on the subject.

Chris Prescott duly arrived, well in time for lunch, which was a light-hearted affair as he gave black, mock-tragic accounts of end-of-term exams, then went with Tash to take Gabriel a cup of coffee. Not long afterwards Tash hugged Imogen convulsively as they said goodbye, promised to send loads of naughty postcards, to use her suncream assiduously, and make herself useful to Mrs Prescott.

Before she got in to the small Citroën parked in the lane Tash ran to the back of the house to say goodbye to Gabriel, then dashed back again to give Imogen a final kiss.

'By the way, you know that rugby shirt Gabriel was wearing this morning?'

'Didn't notice,' lied Imogen.

'Chris did. It may be past its sell-by date but it's definitely a Cambridge University rugby shirt, Stepmama.' Tash grinned cheekily. 'Curiouser and curiouser, *n'est-ce pas*?'

It was quiet in the garden after the car shot off down the lane. Imogen wandered round the lawns and herbaceous borders, admiring Gabriel's handiwork thoughtfully. So he was a Cambridge graduate, was he? An enigma, young Gabriel, one way and another. She shrugged. Whatever he was it was absolutely his own business, nothing to do with her.

She lingered to remove dead heads from the roses and cape daisies, then from the hypericum, which was shedding gold stars down a grassy bank. Anything to postpone returning to the house, which would inevitably feel twice as lonely now that Tash had gone.

On impulse she went to the garden shed and pulled out the mower. She was about to fill it with petrol when a shadow fell across the doorway. She looked up to see Gabriel frowning at her, his slanted eyebrows drawn together in deep disapproval.

'Mrs Lambert, please—leave that to me.'

She straightened. 'Look, Gabriel, I just wanted something to do.'

'Now your stepdaughter's gone?' The slight emphasis on the 'step' was deliberate.

'Yes. Tash is lively company,' she said, wiping her hands with a piece of cotton waste. 'When she goes the house is deadly quiet. So I just thought I'd mow the lawn.' She managed a smile. 'That much, at least, I know how to do.'

He waved a hand at a large box of lawn fertiliser on the shelf. 'I treated the grass with that this morning. It needs to be left for three days before cutting.'

'Oh.' She sighed, defeated. 'Very well. In that case I'd better find something to do in the house.'

He walked with her as far as the kitchen door. 'Could I have a glass of water, Mrs Lambert?'

She smiled, pleased that he had brought himself to ask for something at last. 'Of course; come in the kitchen and sit down while you drink it.'

He shook his head, staying where he was in the doorway as she ran water into an ice-filled glass. 'My boots are covered in earth. Thank you.' He took the glass from her and drank deeply. 'I needed that. It's thirsty work in your little wilderness out there. I've done some surface clearing, but I'll attack it properly with the brush-cutter tomorrow.'

'Brush-cutter?'

He nodded. 'We've got one at home. I'll bring it with me.'

Imogen began stacking a tray with dishes at the table. 'Your garden must be very well-equipped—or do you keep machinery like that for clients' gardens?'

He nodded, then drained the glass. 'I must get on. Thanks for the water.'

She glanced at the kitchen clock. 'I'll bring you some tea in an hour.'

'Thank you.' Black-lashed grey eyes looked very directly into hers. 'Why did you introduce Miss Lambert as your daughter yesterday?'

Startled by the sudden descent into the personal, Imogen found herself stammering in explanation. 'I— I think of her that way, I suppose. She was still a little girl when I first met her. Her own mother died when she was tiny, so I'm the next best thing to a mother she's got.'

'It seems a happy arrangement.'

'It is, thankfully. We've always got on together. Our recent—' Imogen faltered again for a moment '—our recent loss has brought us even closer together.'

'I'm glad. But I don't think you're being completely honest,' he went on relentlessly. 'You told *me* she was your daughter to put me at a distance, underline the gap between us. Perhaps my offerings of chairs and tea yesterday made you afraid I'd begun to encroach, get too familiar.' His face darkened. 'Let's get this straight, Mrs Lambert; if you don't want me around just say so.'

She stared at him, aghast. This kind of problem had never arisen with the builder's men. But then, none of the builder's men had been remotely like Gabriel. Which was the root of the problem. Gabriel was young, obviously intelligent, with a physical attraction few women would be immune to.

'I've obviously offended you. I'm sorry,' she said stiffly. Then she lifted her chin and met the smoke-dark eyes head-on. 'I'm a widow, living alone. Because of Tash's teasing when she saw you on the cricket pitch it suddenly occurred to me that you might misunderstand if I was too—too friendly.'

'I understand all too well,' he said caustically, his eyes darkening. 'I've known all along that to you I'm just a local lad with long hair and a motorbike who happens to have time to spare for your garden. You took it for granted that I listened to heavy metal on my Walkman, that I'd need money for the weekend to make hay with the local girls, in short that I'm below your touch—'

'That's not true!' she said indignantly. 'I plead guilty about the music bit, but my problem was the fact that—that—'

'I can't hide how much I'm attracted to you,' he said baldly, taking her breath away. 'There's not much I can do about that— but don't let it worry you, Mrs Lambert. I promise I'll keep to my side of the fence. After this week you need never see me again.' He turned on his heel and strode back through the laurel hedge and out of sight into the wood.

Imogen stared after him, poleaxed. After a while she pulled herself together and applied herself, dazed, to the washing-up. Her hands automatically rinsed and wiped while her brain went round in circles. How did she deal with Gabriel from now on? If he had been a few years older she would have welcomed his declaration wholeheartedly. After months in limbo after Philip's death it was good to see a light at the end of the tunnel.

But Gabriel was rather too bright a light to cope with. As Tash had said, he was a star. But stars were light-years away, while Gabriel was both too close for comfort and too far out of reach.

CHAPTER FIVE

IMOGEN passed a lonely, restless evening once Gabriel left. After working herself into a state of nerves before taking him his afternoon tea it had been an anti-climax when he thanked her formally, took the cup and turned away, making it plain that he preferred to drink his tea alone. And later he'd left his mug on the kitchen window-ledge when she was somewhere else in the house, and gone off for the day without saying goodbye.

He might, she thought, depressed, not even come back tomorrow in the circumstances. The prospect dismayed her so much that she took a tray loaded with kettle and tea things up to her bedroom later, fully expecting a sleepless night. A long session of Jane Austen soothed her to sleep eventually, however, but she woke early to a dark cloud that was nothing to do with the flawless weather outside.

She took her time over getting up. She lingered in the bath with a book, then dawdled over the breakfast-table with a pot of coffee. By the time Gabriel put in an appearance she was so certain that he wouldn't come that she stared at him blankly when he appeared in the open kitchen doorway.

'Good morning, Mrs Lambert,' he said, just as he always did.

'Good morning, Gabriel. I didn't expect to see you this morning,' she said, taking the war into the enemy's camp.

He looked at her impassively. 'I said I'd do my best to tidy up your garden, so, weather permitting, that's what I'll do.'

She nodded stiffly, very much on her dignity. 'How kind.'

'Not at all,' he returned, equally distant. 'I've brought the brush-cutter, so unless there's anything you'd prefer me to do I'll get on with clearing the little wilderness.'

'Little wilderness', thought Imogen as he strode off. A good description of her life for the time being, until Tash came back from France. She gazed through the open door at the garden, at the bright flowers in the beds bordering the lawn.

The sunlight poured like filtered gold through the trees along the lane, and suddenly she felt ashamed. So many people would have given anything to be in her shoes—a beautiful little house, the qualifications to earn enough money to hold on to it, as well as the blessing of an affectionate girl like Tash. It was time—high time—that she stopped feeling sorry for herself. She'd start looking for a job—one with a salary sufficient to provide for both a flat in London and Beech Cottage, now that she knew Tash was so attached to the place.

She longed to go out for the day, but the thought of being shut up in the car was unbearable as the temperature mounted to the nineties. By midday the heat was intense, and she was very glad that Gabriel was working in the wild section under the trees. She reminded herself to ask him, once they were on better terms again, when to plant foxgloves there, and anything else that thrived in shaded woodland.

At lunchtime he appeared in the doorway as she was making herself a sandwich. 'Mrs Lambert, I thought I'd save you a trip to the shed. I'm keeping to the shade to eat my lunch today.'

'In that case I'll give you your coffee now,' she said, 'unless you'd prefer a cold drink?'

He mopped his sweating forehead with the bandanna he'd taken off. 'I'll have a glass of water first, please, but I'll never say no to your coffee.'

She filled a glass and handed it to him. 'It's very hot today. Won't you take a break and drink the coffee in here?'

He shook his head. 'I think not. Thanks just the same—Mrs Lambert,' he added deliberately.

'As you wish,' she said coolly, and poured coffee into the large mug she'd begun to think of as his.

He thanked her, took the mug, and with an inclination of his dark, glossy head went back to the shady wilderness beyond the laurels.

By mid-afternoon the atmosphere was so thick and sultry that Imogen was plagued by foreboding, coupled with the usual dull headache which presaged thunder. She took him some tea, and said goodbye for the day.

'I think we're shaping up for a storm so I'm keeping a low profile indoors, nursing a headache. I loathe thunderstorms,' she said by way of an explanation.

He looked concerned. 'Is there anything I can do?'

'No. Thanks just the same. Goodbye, Gabriel.'

'I'll see you in the morning,' he said, frowning. 'I hope you feel better soon.'

She sighed. 'I will once the storm's over. I suppose there's no chance this one will pass us by?'

He cast a glance at the leaden clouds massing on the horizon. 'Afraid not.' He hesitated. 'Would you like me to stay?'

Although there was nothing she wanted more she shook her throbbing head. 'No, of course not. I'll be fine. If I were you I'd get off home now, before the rain comes.'

He nodded. 'Perhaps I will. I'll stow the brush-cutter in the shed until tomorrow. I don't fancy juggling with it on the bike in a downpour. And by the way, the way things are going, I reckon I'll be all finished by Thursday, so we'll make that my last day.'

As the evening wore on Imogen paced the rooms of the cottage like a captive tigress. She longed for the storm to break and get it over with, at the same time hoping that it would hold off as long as possible—even bypass Abbots Munden altogether. But the menacing sky grew greenish dark, and the air was thick and heavy. She found it hard to breathe as she turned on the lights to counteract the gloom.

Her head pounded and her stomach churned with apprehension. There was no closet under the stairs to hide in as her grandmother had done. The stairs at Beech Cottage were an open, ladder-like affair of worn wood, with a Pembroke table below them under a mirror Philip had bought her in Venice.

Suddenly the world exploded. A hissing fork of lightning struck the middle of the lawn as the storm broke with an ear-splitting crack of thunder which shook the house. Imogen gave a screech of terror and rushed to draw the curtains as one crack of thunder succeeded another in a terrifying cacophony of sound in counterpoint to the lightning.

She raced upstairs to close her bedroom windows, wincing as the lights flickered ominously with each lightning flash. Then the rain came, drumming down with a force which brought a strong, nutty smell from the steaming earth outside, and she felt marginally better. Rain would relieve the heat and put an end to the storm more quickly, she consoled herself, and returned downstairs to roam from room to room.

It seemed like hours before the storm began to lessen at last. When Imogen could count to ten between each flash of lightning and the crack of thunder which followed she felt confident enough to make a pot of coffee. In the act of filling a mug she almost dropped the pot as from the kitchen window she saw lightning fork through a tree in the lane, splitting it in half. A great crash of thunder shook the cottage to its foundations and the lights went out.

She stood rooted to the spot, her heart thumping so loudly in her chest that it was a moment or two before she realised that someone was hammering on the kitchen door.

'Mrs Lambert? *Imogen*! Are you all right?'

Gabriel's voice flooded her with such relief that her knees shook as she made for the door to throw it open. A tall shape in dripping oilskins stood there like some primeval figure risen from the deep as a lightning flash outlined him in fire.

'Gabriel!' she cried hoarsely. 'Why—how—?'

He thrust her back into the room as thunder cracked and lightning hissed again somewhere near by. 'When it got so bad I was worried about you,' he said, panting, and stripped off his waterproof by the door. 'So I got the car and drove over to make sure you were all right. I'm bloody glad I did now—I saw lightning strike the tree outside. It's blocking the lane so I had to leave the car. I ran the last hundred yards faster than the Olympic record.'

'Athletics as well as rugby?' she said a little wildly.

'Sorry—not at my best tonight. Feeble to be so scared. But it was so good of you to come—I was beginning to calm down a bit, even made some coffee, then the tree went up in flames and the lights went out. It was the last *straw*!'

Her voice cracked on the last and he took her by the elbows, holding her steadily in an impersonal grasp. 'I bet there are a lot of frightened people in the village tonight. Now, first of all, do you have a torch? Like a fool I left mine in the car—but don't worry, I can go back and fetch it if you don't.'

She blenched as another crack of thunder shook the house. 'No! Don't go out there. There's a torch on the shelf in the broom cupboard.'

Philip Lambert, forewarned by colleagues with houses in the country, had stocked the cupboard shelf with such necessities as batteries, a supply of candles and matches as well as a torch.

'Good,' said Gabriel in approval as thunder rolled overhead. 'It may be hours before the electricity comes on again, so "let there be light".'

He shone the torch for her to find saucers in one of the cupboards. Within seconds the kitchen was transformed by the soft light of half a dozen candles, set at strategic points round the room.

'Keep the candles in one place and use the torch for moving from room to room,' he instructed, inspecting the batteries by candlelight. 'And if these fit your transistor you can even listen to one of the audio books.'

She gazed at the clear-cut profile limned in candlelight, and felt a rush of emotion that was not entirely gratitude. 'Thank you, Gabriel,' she said unsteadily. 'It was very good of you to turn out on a night like this. I'm deeply grateful. Dry your hair; it's very wet.'

'That won't kill me.' He turned, the light behind him so that she couldn't see his face. 'My brother's biking gear covered the rest.'

'I'm glad you didn't come on the motorbike tonight!' she said with a shudder. 'You could have been struck by lightning.'

'I was worried about you, alone here, and frightened.' He moved towards her. 'Normally you seem so together and in control. It got to me that you were human after all, with something you were actually afraid of.'

'I'm afraid of a lot of things,' she said in a constricted voice. Not least of being alone here in the candlelight with Gabriel, with the storm still raging overhead and the air between them full of electricity of a very different kind.

'Now I know you're all right I'd better go,' he said huskily.

She looked at him in appeal. 'Couldn't you stay a little?' she asked. 'At least until the storm stops circling round like this. Every time I think it's over it comes back.'

As if to illustrate her words another vivid lightning flash lit the room, thunder cracked overhead and she gasped and smothered a scream with her clenched fist against her mouth. He leapt across the room and took her in his arms, holding her trembling body close against his.

'Don't!' he said against her hair. 'There's nothing to be afraid of.'

'Yes, there is,' she said hoarsely, her face buried against his chest. 'I'm afraid of *this*.'

'I won't hurt you,' he said fiercely, and tipped her face up to his. 'Imogen, look at me. If it hadn't been for the storm I'd never have come back tonight. But I wanted to. God, how I wanted to. Why do you think I came back in the evenings before? I brought you things as an excuse just to see you again, talk to you.

'From the moment we met you're all I've thought about. I never believed you'd turn up at the cricket match. You said you had someone coming so I assumed it was some man, and I was murderous with jealousy. Then you arrived with Natasha and I felt such a rush of adrenalin that I could have taken on the world.'

He cupped a long hand under her chin, looking deep into her eyes as he tightened an arm round her. 'And don't pretend this is all on my side, because I can feel your heart beating against mine like a sledgehammer.'

She stared up at the hollows and planes of his face, thrown into relief in the flickering light of the candles. 'Gabriel, this is madness—'

'Because I'm the gardener and you're the lady of the house?' He paused as she shook her head in swift repudiation. 'Then why?'

Her lids dropped to hide her eyes. 'Lots of reasons—age, propriety, widowhood. And we live in a village where everyone knows everyone else's business—'

'That's nonsense!' he broke in roughly, locking both arms round her. 'I don't have a wife. And your husband died almost a year ago—no one expects you to mourn forever.' His arms dropped away and he stepped back suddenly, his face bleak in the soft light. 'Unless you loved him so much that you can't bear the thought of any other man. If that's the case—'

'It's not the case at all,' she cried, throwing the words like arrows. 'I loved Philip, and I do mourn him.' Suddenly her secret became unbearable. 'But I still feel so *angry* with him under the grief.'

'Angry?'

She nodded. 'Because of the way he died.'

'I heard he had an accident on a wet night—his car hit a tree.'

'That's right. Only it wasn't an accident. He drove his car deliberately off the road, down an embankment into a whole row of trees. The police said he was killed instantly, thank God. No one else was involved, and it was assumed that he must have lost control in torrential rain, driving too fast as usual. But he left me a letter so I know differently.' She stopped suddenly, appalled. 'Gabriel, I'm sorry—the storm's addled my brain. I shouldn't be telling you this.'

'Does anyone else know?' he asked, taking her hands in his.

'No. I destroyed the letter.' Tears began to stream down her face. 'Natasha must never know. She worshipped her father.'

Gabriel pulled her close again, but this time there was nothing sexual in the embrace. He held her lightly, a hand smoothing over her hair as her tears soaked his shirt. 'No one will know from me,' he said with emphasis.

'I've never told a soul,' she whispered brokenly. 'Everyone thinks I can't get over Philip's death. And in a way they're right. I just can't forgive him for taking his own life.'

Gabriel put her away from him a little, his face grim. 'I don't understand. Why did he commit suicide when he had a beautiful young wife like you? Not to mention a daughter.'

'It's a long story,' she said wearily.

He thrust a hand towards the nearest candle to look at his watch. 'It's only a little after eleven. I'm not leaving you here alone until the storm's over. So let it all out, Imogen. I'll never repeat a word of it and you'll feel a whole lot better afterwards.'

She smiled faintly. 'You're very masterful all of a sudden.'

'Not all of a sudden.' He smiled, his teeth gleaming white in the half-light. 'I try to keep my place when I'm doing your gardening, of course. But out of working hours I tend to revert to type—as you noticed just now.'

She flushed, unseen in the candlelight. 'All right, then, Gabriel. Perhaps you're right. Sharing my secret might be just what I need.'

'Before you start, do you have any brandy?'

'Yes, of course—I'll get you some.'

'For you, not me. You look exhausted.'

'Nervous strain,' she returned, and picked up two saucers. 'Bring the other candles into the sitting-room. We might as well sit in comfort—the brandy's in there anyway.'

Gabriel set a row of candles below the triple mirror over the fireplace. He watched as she took two glasses from a corner cabinet, then poured from a decanter on a table between the windows. The storm muttered and growled all around them but her primeval fear had gone. And so had her headache, she discovered, surprised, as she curled up in a corner of the sofa.

Gabriel perched on one of the buttoned leather corners of the club fender and she looked her fill at him in the candlelight's reflected glow, no longer caring if he misinterpreted the pleasure she took in the mere sight of him. His overlong hair was damp and curling from the sprint through the rain, but his clothes were utterly right on him—a fawn linen shirt, an expensive, woven leather belt at the waist of thin beige cotton trousers, which despite their casual cut fitted him so well that they might have been made for him.

'That's a very long, analytical look,' he said gravely.

'I was reflecting on your enigmatic qualities,' she said truthfully. 'A contradiction in terms in some ways. A mystery man.'

'No mystery really,' he said, and raised his glass to her. 'Drink some brandy. You'll feel better.'

She sipped cautiously, the spirit warming her but otherwise no more to her taste than it ever was. 'Where shall I begin?' she asked.

'The beginning is usually best.' His eyes gleamed between his black lashes and Imogen smiled slowly in response.

'Very well. Once upon a time I applied for the post of personal assistant to the vice-chairman of a prestigious international bank.'

Her eyes grew introspective as she remembered the day she'd been shown into Philip's office. Her qualifications and office skills had already been thoroughly tested and vetted by the terrifying personnel director before she was shown into the vice-chairman's presence.

Philip Lambert, slim, fair, with piercing blue eyes, had jumped to his feet to shake her hand. And at once she had known that the job was hers. Something in the way he had spoken when he'd gone through the motions of asking about her experience and qualifications told her, without words, that in the end she would be his choice, no matter how many candidates he interviewed.

'We got on together from the first,' she said, staring down into the amber liquid in her glass. 'I loved the job, too. It was demanding and varied; I met so many interesting people, and the salary was far more than I'd ever earned before. But, more important than any of that, I worked for Philip Lambert. I liked him on sight, and grew to love him in time.'

'And was this reciprocated?' asked Gabriel.

'Yes,' she said simply.

There was nothing rushed in the relationship. She'd worked for Philip for almost a year before he asked her out to dinner one night. And it was another six months before they became lovers. Because of Natasha there was no question of them living together, and it wasn't long before Philip proposed marriage. Imogen was twenty-seven and Philip fifty-two, but because of his blond curly hair, blue eyes and slim, wiry physique he looked a good ten years younger.

'Despite the difference in age we enjoyed a very— close relationship,' she went on without inflexion. 'Natasha and I got on like a house on fire; even her mother's parents liked me, and I them. I could hardly believe my good fortune.

'Then, a couple of years ago, Philip, the archetypal workaholic, suffered a slight stoke. It was fleeting and left him unimpaired in every way, but it brought him up short, decided him to retire. Which meant that I had to resign too, of course. Not that I minded. But before he actually left the bank he suffered another stroke, rather more serious this time. It was at this point that he decided to buy this place in the country for weekends. Neither of us wanted country life on a permanent basis, but Philip fancied a picturesque little retreat as a change from the pace of city life.'

Then things had begun to change. After the second stroke his sex-drive diminished almost to non-existence. It humiliated and infuriated him, no matter how much Imogen assured him that it made no difference to her love for him. His consultant laid the law down, told him that he had to rethink his life, that another stroke could finish him if he didn't cut out smoking, alcohol, keep to a sensible diet, and walk more, instead of speeding everywhere in his beloved classic Jensen.

Imogen made it passionately clear to her husband that the new way of life would be no sacrifice on her part. She was proud and glad to do anything in the world for him, and lectured him on the subject of not having to get ill at all if he just behaved sensibly and took the consultant's advice.

'This, however, was something Philip just couldn't do.' She shrugged. 'A day at a time was as long as he could stick it here at the cottage. In fact he hardly came here at all. The suggestion that we live here permanently and settle to a quiet life in the country appalled him.'

So eventually, with the foresight and attention to detail which had characterised him, Philip put his life in order as a prelude to death. He settled a comfortable allowance on Natasha, put the London house up for sale and made over the cottage to Imogen. For six months, which they spent in London while people came to look over the town house, he cleverly managed to convince his wife that he'd acceded to her pleas to be sensible, that he was resigned to leading a quiet life.

They would have one week of city high life to celebrate, he told her—dine, dance, go to the theatre, throw a fabulous farewell party—and then settle down to rural peace and quiet. Imogen, believing him implicitly, arranged everything for him with her usual efficiency, just as she'd always done.

Then, two days after the brilliantly successful party, he sent her ahead to the cottage, saying that he'd drive down the next day. But he never arrived. In the early hours of the following night, with a storm raging overhead and rain coming down in torrents, his car plunged over an embankment and down into a copse of trees. The autopsy confirmed that the impact killed him instantly, and that he'd been drinking heavily.

'So why didn't you believe it was an accident?' asked Gabriel, after a long pause.

'I received a letter from him the day after,' she said bleakly. 'Instructions about the will and so on. He told me life wasn't worth living with the prospect of another stroke hanging over him like the sword of Damocles. Philip had always looked young for his age. He couldn't cope with growing old and ill, and—I suspect most of all—being unable to make love.

'The joke of it is that I didn't care about that. I would have done anything in the world for him. He just couldn't accept my sacrifice, he wrote. His plan was to drive to a deserted hillside lay-by in the small hours, down a bottle of whisky, and, when no one was about, speed off the road into oblivion. He asked me to look after his daughter, told me he loved me too much to tie me to an impotent invalid, and instructed me to burn the letter the moment I'd read it. Tash must never know he'd committed suicide.'

Gabriel crossed the space between them in a sudden, swift movement, and went down on his knees in front of her. He took her glass from her and set it down on the table, then grasped both her ice-cold hands in his.

'Is that why you can't bear storms?' he asked with compassion. 'Because your husband died on a night like this?'

'It's part of it.' She stared down at their hands. 'I was nervous of storms before. But I spent an entire night waiting through one for Philip to come home, then the police arrived instead to tell me he was dead.' She breathed in deeply. 'You can see why I get a bit strung up.'

Suddenly the relief of telling someone, of sharing the secret that had weighed so heavily on her for the past year, released the lock that she kept on her emotions. Tears began to slide down her face, her shoulders shook and Gabriel released her hands. In one movement he leapt up to sit beside her and take her into his arms, smoothing her head against his shoulder.

'Cry!' he ordered, and Imogen, helpless suddenly to do anything else, obeyed him. He held her close, stroking her hair and murmuring indistinct words of comfort as the hot salt tears cleansed her anger away at last.

'Better now?' he asked eventually, then put her away from him gently and got up, taking the torch into the kitchen.

She sat limply, swollen-eyed, her hair all over the place, scarcely able to believe that she'd shared her secret with someone who'd been a stranger only a week before. She looked up as he returned with a handful of dampened kitchen paper and a clean kitchen towel.

She mopped herself up, then gave him a shaky smile. 'Sorry I cried all over you, Gabriel. You didn't know what you were letting yourself in for when you offered to tidy my garden.'

He shook his handsome head, his eyes gleaming in the candlelight. 'On the contrary, I knew exactly what I was doing.'

She frowned. 'What do you mean?'

'I looked up from digging a trench for Sam Harding and saw a vision in a floating sort of dress and a wide straw hat. I couldn't see those beautiful green eyes behind the sunglasses, but one look at you and I was ready to do whatever it was that brought you there that day.'

'And you have,' she said, looking away. 'The garden's a picture. You've introduced me to the delights of the talking book—'

'That's not the only delight I'd like to share with you,' he broke in, a note in his voice which dried her mouth. 'Don't look like that. I won't take advantage of your vulnerability right now.'

'Does that mean you'll try to take advantage of it some time in the future?' she countered tartly.

He grinned. 'That's better. The spirit's back.'

'True. And because it is,' said Imogen firmly, 'there's one barrier between us you'd better know I find totally insurmountable—and it's nothing to do with the employer-employee factor.'

'What is it, then?'

'Age.' She looked at him very steadily. 'I know— none better—that an age-gap in a relationship can present problems. I could cope when the man was older than me. But, Gabriel, I could never get involved—even in the most superficial way—with a man a lot younger than myself. Like you.'

'Just how old do you think I am?' he demanded.

'I don't know. And it doesn't matter, because once you leave on Thursday we probably won't meet again.'

'I wouldn't count on it,' he said forcefully, and reached down to pull her up on her feet. 'Shall I tell you why?' he demanded, keeping hold of her hands.

'Gabriel—' But whatever else she intended to say was lost as his arms closed around her and his mouth took hers, and she yielded to the sheer pleasure of his kiss, allowing herself the glorious danger of it just this one time.

It was so good to feel hard male arms around her, to feel a muscular young body grow taut and heated as it came into contact with her own. After the tears and cathartic effect of her confession Imogen's emotions were out of kilter. Her senses were set adrift by the touch of hands surprisingly subtle and sensitive in their caresses. He made love to her with a passionate tenderness which coaxed and inflamed and brought her with shocking speed to a point where she wanted nothing more in the world than to let him love her as she'd never been loved before.

It was Gabriel who wrenched away, Gabriel who turned his back to her, his fists clenched, unaware that, within minutes, his urgency had restored the self-esteem missing from Imogen from the moment she'd opened the letter Philip had written before he died.

'I'm sorry,' he said hoarsely, still with his back turned. 'I said I wouldn't so somehow—Lord knows how—I've let you go. I've wanted to make love to you from the moment I laid eyes on you, Imogen, but that's no excuse. Tonight, believe it or not, my intentions were of the purest, in theory. But something went wrong.'

'On the contrary, it went very right,' she said simply.

He spun round, his eyes incredulous. 'You mean that?'

She nodded, pushing her hair back from her face. 'I'm only human, Gabriel. It was a healing process to have you kiss me, good to know you wanted me in such a straightforward, uncomplicated sort of way.'

He gave a snort of laughter. 'Uncomplicated! I kissed you in desperation, Imogen, just in case I never got the opportunity again, and now I'm bloody sorry I did because I want to kiss you again, and I'm going to go on wanting to. I want to make love to you in every way there is, and maybe a few more ways we could find out in the process.'

She took in a deep, shaky breath. 'Gabriel, it can't happen. After tonight I know I can get over the trauma of Philip's death. And you made that possible for me. I'm more grateful than you'll ever know.' She made a fierce little gesture. 'And I won't deny that I would like to make love with you. But I can't emerge from one emotional minefield to plunge straight into another.'

His eyes smouldered. 'If I've helped I suppose it's some reward. Not the one I want!' he added roughly. 'But if it means that life will be easier for you in future, Imogen, then I must be content with that—for now.' He turned away. 'I don't want to go, but I suppose I'd better get home. Will you be all right?'

'Yes,' she said with conviction. 'I'll be fine. Maybe I won't even be so afraid of thunderstorms from now on.'

'Tell me,' he said as they took the candles into the kitchen, 'when you said you felt anger towards Philip was that because he rejected your sacrifice?'

'Partly.' Her eyes flashed. 'But the main reason is that Philip couldn't take his life without letting me know. He needed me to admire his action for the grand gesture he believed it to be. And he really didn't have to ask me to take care of Tash!' she added with passion. 'He *knew* I adored his child as if she were my own. I've been so angry, Gabriel, because I didn't *want* the burden of knowing that he had killed himself. If he loved me as much as he said he did he shouldn't have told me.'

'Bloody right he shouldn't,' said Gabriel savagely, and pulled her into his arms, kissing her hard, his embrace a mixture of heat and consolation and such unadulterated male urgency that she responded to it, her hands sliding into the long, dark hair. The kiss deepened, grew hot and urgent: Then the lights came on and brought them back to earth.

Imogen broke away from him hurriedly, hideously conscious now of her swollen eyes and tumbled hair in light that was cruel after that of the soft, flattering candles.

'No,' he said and pulled her back against him. 'Come here. You look warm and untidy and totally irresistible. But if you prefer—' He reached out and switched off the overhead light, then held her close, one hand tipping up her chin so that his mouth was just a fraction away from hers. 'After tonight this may never happen again,' he said, his voice deepening in a way which trickled a shiver of response down her spine. 'I don't understand why—none of your reasons sound good to me.'

'No—' she began, but Gabriel wasn't listening, too absorbed in the pleasure of their communing mouths and tongues, the shape of her shoulders under his caressing hand, which slid up into her hair and held her head immovable as his free hand slid lower to press her against him. A great bolt of mutual desire shot through them both, fiercer than any of the lightning flashes during the storm. She gasped and held him close, drowning in a hot, turbulent sea of physical longing.

When he drew away at last he was breathing heavily, far more so than after his sprint through the storm. 'I don't want to go,' he said hoarsely, 'and you know I don't. I'd ask Imogen to let me stay, but Mrs Lambert of Beech Cottage would feel duty-bound to refuse.' His fingers closed cruelly on the hand he was holding. 'But tell me, Imogen, if only for charity's sake, that you'd *like* me to stay.'

She gave a wry, unsteady little laugh. 'Oh, yes, Gabriel,' she said raggedly, 'I'd like you to stay. For all kinds of reasons I'd like you to stay.'

His face softened in the guttering candlelight. 'After Thursday—after I finish working for you—I'll bring the subject up again. I'll regroup my forces and come back to conquer. In the meantime, I'll see you in the morning.' He bent to pick up the waterproof.

'I hope your brother isn't missing that on his dig,' she said.

'Hector's notorious for losing his belongings,' he said as he shrugged the large windproof parka over his head. 'Useful for me—I borrow some of his more disreputable cast-offs to work in.'

'Is the rugby shirt his?' she couldn't help asking.

'Yes—discarded after his first year at King's. He grew,' he added with a grin.

'So Hector was at Cambridge?' she said lightly.

'Still is. Reading archaeology, playing rugby, chasing girls, and, in his spare time, turning up bits of Roman mosaic floor in a Norfolk field. But enough about Hector. Concentrate on me.' He kissed her swiftly. 'Goodnight. And don't worry if you sleep late in the morning. I'll get on with the gardening very quietly, I promise. Oh, by the way,' he added, 'I'll be leaving at lunchtime tomorrow. Promised to fetch someone from London.'

'Right,' she said, dying to ask who the someone was but determined not to. 'Gabriel?'

He turned sharply in the open doorway. 'Yes?'

'Thank you.'

'For what, exactly?'

'For appearing in my hour of need—for thinking of me when the storm broke.'

'I think of you all the time,' he retorted, his eyes holding hers.

She smiled shakily. 'A habit you'd better break.'

'I doubt if I can. Not after tonight.'

'Gabriel—'

'Don't say any more,' he broke in. 'And, in case you're worried, I shan't appear on your doorstep in the morning in an encroaching manner. Gabriel the knight errant will revert to Gabriel the gardener by tomorrow, I promise.'

She smiled. 'Will he, now? Clever lad, this Gabriel.'

'Not really.' His face shadowed. 'In fact, I've been incredibly stupid in one instance.' He shrugged ruefully. 'Too late now.'

'You mean you regret making love to me?' she said quickly.

He smiled, his eyes gleaming in the shimmer of dying candlelight. 'You know very well, Imogen, that making love to you was just as perfect as I knew it would be. Only one drawback to it.'

'Oh?'

His smile widened. 'It's so addictive that I'm having the devil's own job keeping my distance right this minute. Goodnight, darling, sleep well.' He raised a hand and went out into the pouring rain, closing the door firmly behind him.

Imogen bolted the door as if in a dream, blew out the candles, then drifted up the creaking stairs, Gabriel's endearment echoing in her head all through the process of taking herself to bed—a hypnotic mantra that lulled her to sleep the moment her head touched the pillow.

CHAPTER SIX

TRUE to his word, next morning Gabriel made no attempt to cash in on the experiences of the night. When he arrived his smile was warm as he handed her a bag of newly picked vegetables, but one look into his eyes told Imogen that there was no way that either of them could pretend nothing had happened between them.

'I'd better let the grass dry after all that rain,' he said as he leaned in the doorway drinking the coffee that she had handed him. 'I'll do some more weeding, leave the place as easy as possible for you to cope with yourself.'

Her face shadowed. After tomorrow he'd be gone. 'Do you have another job to go to?'

He hesitated for a moment, then nodded. 'Yes, I do. I've had a word with Sam Harding, by the way,' he added quickly. 'His hand's healed now. He'll spare you a few hours in the garden now and then, if you like.'

She smiled radiantly. 'I like very much! Thank you.' She smiled ruefully. 'What an angel you've been— Gabriel! You've done some rather radical sorting out in my life since we first met.' Then, abandoning all pretence of keeping to their usual relationship, she said quietly, 'I'll miss you. Badly.'

For a moment she thought that he would leap across the kitchen and take her in his arms, but he clenched his fists and quite visibly forced himself to stay where

he was. 'If you want me to keep to my role of gardener, Mrs Lambert, ma'am, it might be easier if you
didn't say things like that. Not yet, anyway.'

'Not yet?'

'Until after tomorrow!' He gave her an enigmatic
smile, put his mug on the counter and went off to
collect his tools.

After tomorrow, mused Imogen as she tried to find
things to occupy her that morning. After little more
than a week of having Gabriel around it was horri-
fyingly difficult to imagine life without him. She
would miss watching his energetic conquest of her
unruly garden. Unfortunately the garden wasn't the
only thing he'd conquered. Just to see him leaning in
the doorway this morning had been enough to
transform her day.

She hugged her arms across her chest in her
bedroom, glaring at the angels on the headboard. How
had she let things come to such a pass? Was it her
fate never to fall in love with someone in her own age-
group? Not that wanting Gabriel was a crime. Lots
of women had husbands or lovers years younger than
themselves and were blissfully happy with the
arrangement.

She sighed. If it hadn't been for Tash things could
well have been different, but she'd promised Philip
that she'd take care of his daughter. Taking a young
lover like Gabriel—one who did casual gardening jobs
in Abbots Munden for a living at that—in no way
fitted in with her role *in loco parentis* to Natasha
Lambert.

Gabriel departed from custom for his mid-morning
break. He arrived at the kitchen door as she was

making coffee, his smile a little rueful. 'I couldn't wait any longer.'

'You were thirsty?' she countered, handing him his mug.

'That too,' he admitted, his eyes locked with hers. 'But if you want the truth I couldn't exist another second away from you.'

She knew she should remonstrate, douse his smile with cold disapproval, but it was impossible.

'No protests?' he demanded.

'No. I felt the same.'

A light flared in his eyes, and she saw his hand clench round the mug. 'Imogen, I could just about cope before when you kept me firmly in my place. If you say things like that I won't answer for the consequences.'

'Then I won't,' she said, and lowered the temperature by confiding her intention of getting a job.

He frowned. 'A job? Where?'

'In London, I suppose. I've got contacts there and the salaries are higher. Good PAs with experience are still sought after. I can't spend the rest of my life lotus-eating in Abbots Munden.'

He eyed her intently. 'Does that mean you intend selling this place?'

'I fully intended to,' she admitted. 'But Tash loves it here, so I've had to change my plans. After Philip died she was a very unhappy, insecure little person. It took the combined efforts of her grandparents and me to get her to take up her college place, even. She's glad that she did now. Life at university has been just the antidote to her grief that she needed. But this cottage obviously represents security to her. Because her father chose it, I suppose.'

Gabriel put his mug down and folded his arms. 'Is the job a way to fill up your life? Or—forgive me—do you need the money?'

'Both. The restoration here cost far more than Philip forecast. By the time the builders finish the boundary wall I'll have gone way over budget. I wasn't worried,' she added, 'because I fully intended to sell the cottage, find work again and buy a flat in London. But now that Tash wants me to keep this place on I'll have to rethink a bit.'

'It's too far to commute from here to London every day!'

'I know. And the kind of job I've always had means long hours, so I suppose some kind of bedsitter's the answer, cheap enough to let me keep this place on for weekends and holidays.' She shrugged. 'Not what I had in mind, exactly, but—'

'But you love Tash and you were asked to take care of her, so that's what you'll do.' His smoky gaze was analytical. 'Imogen, you've got a life of your own. Surely Tash wouldn't want you to kill yourself trying to keep this place on for her?'

'I've no intention of doing that,' she said tartly. 'I need occupation. I won't find it here, so it has to be London. Where I belong.'

Gabriel, obviously taking this as a signal to get back to work, thanked her for the coffee rather stiffly and went back to his weeding.

The morning hung heavy for Imogen until lunchtime. She busied herself in the kitchen so that she could look out every few minutes to where he was working, until at last she saw him leap to his feet, strip off his gloves and come sprinting up the path. She met him at the kitchen door, and without a word he took her in his arms and kissed her with a thoroughness that brooked no opposition.

'I know I'm not meant to do that,' he muttered into her hair, 'but wanting you is like breathing. I can't stop.'

She locked her hands round his waist, leaning against him, inhaling the scent of warm, aroused male. 'Shouldn't you be going?' she said, muffled against his chest.

'Yes, I should.' He put her away from him with reluctant, lingering hands. 'Will you be in all day?'

She nodded. 'Why?'

'I'll ring you tonight.' His smile turned her heart over. 'Just to make sure you're all right.' His eyes darkened, then he closed them, shaking his head. 'No,' he said fiercely. 'Don't look at me like that or I'll never go.'

'You said you had someone to collect from London.'

His wide mouth curved in a grimace. 'And I'd better be there on the dot, too,' he said with feeling, and turned to run down the path. 'Talk to you later,' he shouted as he wheeled the Harley-Davidson out into the lane.

The long afternoon, she realised, was a foretaste of what life would be like once Gabriel went on to mow pastures new. And, she tried to convince herself, his departure would put a neat end to a situation which was rapidly getting out of hand. There was no future for either of them. The brief summer idyll would be over. And with this uppermost in her mind she got out her laptop and began writing letters of application for the handful of suitable posts that she'd cut from the papers.

When the phone rang as she was getting out of the bath that evening she ran to pick it up, her hair dripping into her insecure towel as she said a breathless hello.

'What *have* you been doing, Stepmama?' mocked Tash's voice. 'Training for a marathon, or have you just torn yourself from the arms of your lover?'

Imogen, unseen, blushed to the roots of her wet hair. 'Tash! How are you? It's good to hear your voice.'

'I'm great. All round and brown like a bun, and the farmhouse here is fabulous. Chris's room-mate at Exeter arrived yesterday, and the four of us had a brilliant time by the river today in a leaky old punt.' Tash paused for breath. 'Anyway, enough about me. How's you? Is that gorgeous hunk of yours still slaving in the garden?'

'I'm fine, and Gabriel finishes slaving tomorrow.' She changed the subject hastily, asking about the holiday, content to let Tash chatter away about her activities until her money ran out.

She spent a long time afterwards brushing her new haircut into perfect shape before making up her face with care. No good letting herself go just because she was alone, she told herself. Afterwards she ate a frugal supper of cheese and salad at the kitchen table, with a gory thriller propped up against the coffee-pot as she waited for the call which never came. When darkness fell she was slumped in front of the television, trying to get interested in a film she'd seen before. At last she turned it off and stared at the blank screen. Gabriel wasn't going to ring after all and it was time she stopped behaving like a lovesick schoolgirl.

It was something new in her life. Her previous relationships—friendly, unimportant affairs before Philip—had been pleasant and painless. And with Philip himself it had been very different from this— no agonising and guilt and hot, illicit desires that she couldn't control, just a steady, unswerving kind of love she'd believed would last forever. With Gabriel she had no expectations beyond tomorrow afternoon.

Imogen was so lost in gloom at the prospect that the light tap on the window brought her, startled, to her feet, her heart turning somersaults as she saw Gabriel smiling at her through the glass. She ran to the kitchen. With trembling hands she shot the bolts on the door, opening it wide as he raced round the house towards her, and the next moment they were in each other's arms, submerged in a kiss that went on and on, his arms like steel bands around her as he backed her into the house.

Her hands locked round his neck as though she'd never let him go, and, without taking his mouth from hers, Gabriel reached behind him to bolt the door. Then he picked her up in his arms and carried her through the hall to lay her down on the sofa. He dropped to his knees, a hand at either side of her, and looked deep into her heavy, glittering eyes.

'I rang earlier,' he said, his voice deeper and rougher than she'd ever heard it before. 'You were talking to someone.'

'Tash,' she whispered, her hand smoothing his cheek.

'I didn't try again. Your voice wouldn't have been enough anyway. I needed to touch you, see you look at me just the way you're looking now.' He bent his head and kissed her eyes shut, then moved his mouth slowly over her face, tracing the bone-structure with his lips until they found hers.

At the contact she felt him stiffen. She trembled like an inexperienced teenager as for the first time Gabriel caressed her breasts with shaking hands. All this was so *new*, she thought wildly as fiery sensation coursed through her from his touch.

His passion was hot and forceful and yet all mixed up with some wild kind of wonder as though he couldn't believe what was happening. Which wasn't strange. Neither could she. Philip had been so assured, so practised, so very much the one in control, whereas Gabriel seemed at the mercy of his own senses as he kissed her until both of them were shaking, panting, oblivious to anything other than the force of the passion that held them in such a grip that neither had any control over the inevitable outcome.

Imogen forgot that she was Mrs Lambert of Beech Cottage, that Gabriel was the young man who came to do the garden, that she was older, or he was younger, or whether Tash would disapprove, or anything in the world other than the basic fact that they were a male and female, conquered by the strongest force in nature.

Without questions or answers they rapidly came together with no barrier between them—clothing, age, social or any other. And with no word spoken, when at the last Imogen's desire was so intense that she thought she'd die of it, together they achieved that rare total loss of identity when two became one in the ultimate bliss of sexual fulfilment.

Afterwards she lay with eyes closed on her long, comfortable sofa, Gabriel's arms still locked around her, his hair brushing her face as he buried his own in her neck.

'Darling, I never meant this to happen,' he said against her hot, damp skin. 'At least, not now, not tonight. I'm a normal male animal, and I want you so much that I won't pretend I didn't want it to happen soon. But I was going to wait—'

'And then you couldn't,' she murmured, stroking his hair. 'And neither, as was so flagrantly obvious, could I.'

He raised his head and looked down into her flushed, softened face. He smiled in elation. 'Have you any idea what it did to me to have you respond like that? It was so much what I'd dreamed about and never believed would happen that I lost control.'

'I noticed.'

He laughed, drawing a caressing finger over the planes of her face. 'You want me to apologise?'

'If you're sorry,' she teased.

He gathered her to him in a crushing embrace. 'Sorry? You know very well it's a waking dream for me to have you here like this. Where I've wanted you right from the beginning,' he added, his voice deepening.

She gave a deep sigh. 'Odd, really. In theory I should feel embarrassed.'

'Naked in the arms of the gardener?' He gave a sudden howl of laughter, throwing back his head, and she joined in, both of them suddenly helpless with mirth as they clutched each other close.

'Terribly D. H. Lawrence,' she said unsteadily when they had recovered. 'What *would* the neighbours say?'

'Since your nearest neighbour lives half a mile away the question doesn't arise,' he assured her, then sobered. 'Would that bother you, Imogen? Having someone know I'm here tonight with you—like this?'

She gave it some thought, then nodded slowly. 'Yes. But only because other eyes wouldn't see the magic, Gabriel.'

He looked at her in silence, then slowly he bent his head to hers and kissed her mouth with such tenderness that she felt tears seep beneath her closed lids. 'No man ever received a greater compliment,' he said gruffly. 'Imogen—please—don't cry.'

'I'm not crying—or if I am it's just a little bit.' She smiled up at him. 'It's getting late. You should go. Only this is the part where I *am* embarrassed.'

'Why?'

She flushed beneath his amused gaze. 'I don't remember taking my clothes off, I regret to say. But now I need to dress again, so turn your back.'

Convulsed with laughter, he leapt up and turned away to gather up his own clothes, indulging Imogen in her need to replace her own away from the smoky grey gaze which caused such havoc with her self-possession. She buttoned her white silk shirt over the lace bra she'd had trouble in locating, cinched her wide cotton skirt securely with a plaited leather belt, then turned to find him fully dressed in the pale blue chambray shirt and jeans that she hadn't even noticed earlier in her joy at seeing him.

'There,' he said indulgently. 'Now we're respectable again.'

'Some might argue with that,' she said drily, and he laughed.

'This is the nineties, Mrs Lambert. We're both adult, unattached and inflicted no damage with what happened. Unless you count the great dent in my heart,' he added theatrically, placing his hand on his chest.

She giggled. 'What a ham!'

He leapt across the space between them and seized her round the waist, nuzzling his mouth all over her face. 'Take that back!' he muttered against her mouth.

'Never!' she shrieked, laughing, and, growling menacingly, he bent her back in his arms like a stage villain assaulting the village maiden. Suddenly neither of them was laughing and he pulled her upright into his arms and kissed her with a ferocity she responded to in kind. In seconds the fun and teasing were replaced by a burning, aching need that startled them both. They pulled apart, breathing hard, gazing at each other in utter consternation.

'What do you *do* to me?' said Gabriel hoarsely. 'I've never felt like this. Ever.'

'Neither have I.'

'*Never*, Imogen?'

She met the exultant gaze squarely. 'Never.'

He took in a deep, unsteady breath, then turned blindly and made for the door. 'If I don't go we both know what will happen,' he flung over his shoulder as she followed him. He shot back the bolt and opened the door, gulping in the cool night air like a drowning man. Then he turned to her and took her in his arms very carefully, as though she had 'fragile' written across her forehead. 'I'm going to give you one very chaste goodnight kiss, and then I'm going home to my bed to dream about tonight, and you, and—'

The rest of his words were muffled against her mouth with his kiss, which was neither as careful nor as chaste as he'd intended. Then, wordlessly, he tore himself away from her and ran down the path to the gate without a backward glance, as though one look over his shoulder would draw him straight back to her arms like a magnet.

It was only when Imogen was in bed later, her dreaming eyes on the stars shining through the window, that she realised she'd heard no noise of any engine as Gabriel left, neither Harley nor car. He'd left as he'd arrived—in silence. Was he protecting her reputation, or had he merely felt like a walk? And if so, how far? She still had no idea where he lived.

Tomorrow, she promised herself, trying to compose herself for sleep, she'd feel entitled to ask questions once she handed over his wages and their employer-employee relationship was terminated. After that, she thought, stretching, it was obvious that he meant their relationship to be a much closer one. And she had no quarrel with that. For the time being, until she found work in London and while Tash was safely in France, she'd allow herself the luxury of a young, passionate lover.

It was Gabriel's wish as much as hers, otherwise he wouldn't have come back. There was no storm to-night, other than the storm of passion which had overwhelmed them both. She hadn't even asked if he'd collected his friend. Imogen laughed suddenly in the darkness. There'd been precious little conversation at all. Yet afterwards it had been so good, such fun to laugh together. Fun had been a rare commodity in her life lately.

CHAPTER SEVEN

IMOGEN woke next morning to loud banging on the door and Gabriel's voice shouting her name. She looked at the clock, aghast, and leapt out of bed, shrugging on her dressing-gown to run downstairs and let him in.

'I slept late,' she gasped, pushing her hair back from her shiny face.

'I can see that,' he said, amused, and shut the door behind him. 'So this is how you look in the mornings—no, don't run away.' He caught her as she turned, and drew her into his arms, kissing her protesting mouth. 'Mmm,' he said with relish, rubbing his cheek against her hair. 'I love the feel of you like this, all hot and flustered through this slippery satin thing. You look about seventeen—'

'But I'm not,' she said breathlessly, and pulled away. 'And ladies of advanced years like to gild the lily a bit before they face the day, so make yourself useful. Put the kettle on while I tidy myself up.'

She smiled as she hurried through a shower and put on her flowered cotton jersey dress. Sleeping late meant that she'd had no time to worry about how to face Gabriel this morning. The problem had been solved very thoroughly for her.

When she went downstairs, still flushed but with hair and eyes shining, he had coffee and toast waiting.

'I thought we might celebrate my last day by having breakfast together,' he announced. 'That is,' he added, with mock subservience, 'if it's all right for the lady of the house to fraternise with the gardener.'

'A bit late to object on my part,' Imogen said drily, and helped herself to a piece of toast. 'Though "celebrate" is hardly a tactful word. Do I take it that you're glad to shake the dust of Beech Cottage from your feet?'

He crunched on his own toast, eyeing her thoughtfully. 'Does that mean you're sorry to see me go?'

'Yes,' she said frankly. 'As I've said before, I'll miss you.'

'I'm not leaving the country—merely terminating my employment, darling. Which means that from four o'clock this afternoon our relationship will be less inhibited.'

'It could hardly be less inhibited than it is already!'

Their eyes met.

'Are you sorry?' he asked quickly.

Imogen made no pretence of misunderstanding. 'No. How could I be?'

Gabriel held out his mug for coffee. 'I'm glad. I had time to think once I'd cooled down on the walk home—'

'Why *did* you walk?' she broke in curiously. 'Were you protecting my reputation?'

He looked a little discomfited. 'No, not really. It was a beautiful night, I felt restless, and if the house was in darkness I meant to go away without disturbing you. If I'd come on the Harley you'd have heard me.'

'So on the walk back you had time to think,' she prompted.

'And wonder if you'd have regrets, blame me for making love to you once you were alone.' His mouth twisted. 'It all happened so fast, like a tidal wave—'

'Which swept us both away,' she finished for him, and smiled.

He smiled back in obvious relief, then heaved a great sigh and looked at the kitchen clock. 'I'd much rather sit here with you all day, but before I clock off this afternoon I intend to mow all the lawns, so I'd better get a move on.'

'Right.' She got up and began to clear away. 'By the way, I've got your money ready for you—' She bit her lip, flushing at the look on his face. 'There's no point in getting on your high horse, Gabriel. You've worked hard on the garden for me. Last night is nothing at all to do with that.'

'Let's leave it until four, shall we?' he said crisply, sounding rather different from Gabriel the lover—or Gabriel the gardener.

'As you like. But I just thought you'd like to know it was in cash.'

'Why?' he demanded sharply. 'Even local lads like me have bank accounts.'

She stiffened. 'I meant,' she said very deliberately, 'that you might prefer not to declare the money since this was a one-off payment. Tax-wise, I mean.'

'I know what you meant.' One slanting black eyebrow rose caustically. 'Tut-tut, Mrs Lambert. Fancy encouraging the hired help to cheat! I'd prefer a cheque, please.'

Frowning in dismay, she watched him go off to take the mower from the garden shed. She'd offended him badly. Mention of money after their lovemaking had obviously touched a nerve.

Long before eleven Imogen took coffee to him where he was edging the strip of newly mown lawn furthest from the cottage.

'Are you still angry with me?' she demanded, thrusting the mug at him.

He grinned. 'No. I've worked off all my angst on your grass. It looks better after my attentions, don't you agree?'

All right with her world again, she smiled back. 'The entire garden looks better after your attentions, Gabriel.'

He drank thirstily, eyeing her over the mug. 'Maybe I'm prejudiced, but I think I'd include you, darling, in that. You look thoroughly edible this morning. Though you looked even more so in that green silk thing, with your hair all over the place.'

'I thought we were leaving all that until after four,' she said, then bit her lip, conscious of the invitation in her words.

He laughed and sat down cross-legged on the grass, patting the place beside him. 'Come and talk to me for a minute. I've been working hard; I deserve a reward.'

She dropped down beside him, her wide skirt spread around her. She leaned back on her hands, squinting up at the cloudless blue sky through the branches of the chestnut tree. 'It's a glorious day, so peaceful and quiet—' She stopped short, surprised at Gabriel's muffled curse as a car stopped at the gate.

Imogen got to her feet hastily to greet the woman coming up the garden path. The visitor was tall and vaguely familiar. She had expertly cut short hair, iron-grey like her eyes, and she wore tailored trousers and a crisp striped shirt. She was smiling as she held out her hand.

'Mrs Lambert? I'm Claudia Sargent. How do you do? Forgive the intrusion, but I've got a message for Gabriel here.'

Imogen murmured a polite greeting, her eyes blank as she turned to Gabriel, who was deeply flushed under his tan as, with a muttered word of thanks, he took the portable phone Mrs Sargent held out to him.

'Sorry to come after you, Gabriel—I did telephone but there was no answer, so I just drove straight round, thinking Mrs Lambert must be out.'

Mrs Lambert had been enjoying a cosy interlude with the gardener in the sun, out of range of the telephone, thought Imogen, mortified.

Gabriel muttered something unintelligible, giving Mrs Sargent an urgent look, which she failed to notice in her admiration of the garden.

'My dear Mrs Lambert, Gabriel's done a really splendid job.' She smiled. 'I feel terribly guilty that I haven't been to see you before. I did call once to give my condolences, but you were in London, and just after that my daughter had a baby, you know, and I've been commuting to the States rather a lot. Which is no excuse. How are you, my dear? Are you recovering now from your loss?'

'Yes,' said Imogen. 'Thank you.' She pulled herself together. 'Won't you come in and have some coffee?'

Mrs Sargent shook her head. 'No, thank you; I must get on. I only got back yesterday—there's nothing much to eat in the house so I'd better raid Tom Jennings' shop and lay in some food.' She smiled as Gabriel came back across the lawn from the shed and handed her the telephone. 'Everything sorted, dear? I brought this toy of yours because I was sure you wouldn't want to call Germany on Mrs Lambert's telephone.'

Germany? Imogen stared at Gabriel in astonishment.

'Thank you,' he said, looking hunted. 'I'll see you to your car.'

'No need, darling, I can see you're busy.'

Darling? Imogen felt suddenly cold.

Mrs Sargent had returned her attention to the garden, unaware of the tension she'd created. 'This place had got so run-down with only one old lady living here. You've done marvels, Mrs Lambert—though I did wonder if you'd hold on to Beech Cottage after your husband died.'

'My stepdaughter is so attached to the house that I'm keeping it on,' said Imogen politely, burningly conscious of Gabriel, who was standing straight like a Grenadier Guard on the periphery of her vision.

'I'm glad,' said Mrs Sargent. 'So many people buy up cottages in these parts, do them up, then sell them on. It's nice to know that you intend enjoying the house now that you've made it look so pleasing again.' She turned an appraising eye on Gabriel. 'No wonder you're so thin, my lad.'

Imogen looked blank.

Mrs Sargent smiled. 'I don't suppose Gabriel's told you he puts in an hour or two in my garden before he comes to you, then does a couple more after he gets back in the afternoon?'

'No, he hasn't.' Imogen gave him a saccharine little smile. 'Gabriel is very uncommunicative about himself. Though I have seen his prowess at cricket.'

Mrs Sargent laughed. 'Quite fancied a career as a professional cricketer once.' She peered at him closely. 'You're very flushed. Not coming down with something, are you?'

'No,' he said with obvious effort. 'It's the sun.'

'After the spell in Greece I wouldn't have thought British sun would bother you!'

Imogen felt that, like Alice, she'd somehow got herself on the other side of the mirror. Nothing felt real except for the suspicion sprouting in her mind like a beanstalk.

'Are you sure you won't come in for coffee, Mrs Sargent?' she said cajolingly. 'I don't get many visitors.'

The other woman's face softened. 'In that case I'm sure I can leave the shopping for a while.' She waved a hand at Gabriel. 'Don't just stand there, dear—get on with the grass. They say it's going to rain later.'

He turned away, raking a despairing hand through his hair as Imogen ushered Mrs Sargent into the kitchen.

'Sorry to bring you in this way,' she said, going on through the hall to the sitting-room. 'Because the kitchen door is at the side of the house I tend to use it all the time. I keep the front door locked and bolted. My husband was very security-conscious.'

'Quite right too,' said Mrs Sargent, looking round her in approval. 'At one time one could go out and leave the house open all day without a qualm, but no longer, alas. This is a very charming room,' she added.

'Thank you. It was my first foray into interior decorating,' said Imogen. 'If you'll excuse me for a moment I'll just get some coffee.'

A few minutes later she returned with a tray, complete with Spode cups and silver *sucrier* and cream jug, and biscuits on an oval porcelain dish. Mrs Sargent was at the window, watching Gabriel push the lawnmower at savage speed up and down the main lawn.

'That boy does everything at top speed,' she commented, and sat down in a small armchair covered in buttoned, snuff-coloured velvet.

Imogen poured coffee from a silver pot, added cream at Mrs Sargent's request, offered biscuits, then sat down in her usual corner of the sofa. 'I came round to your house while you were away, on Mr Jennings' advice, Mrs Sargent. He thought Sam Harding might be able to help me.'

'Only Sam had sliced his hand rather badly and you found Gabriel instead.' Mrs Sargent smiled. 'Gabriel's always helped in the garden in his spare time. He likes grubbing about in the earth and growing things as much as I do. Do you like gardening?'

'I do, actually. My main problem was ignorance. I've lived in a town all my life, never had a garden, so I didn't know weeds from plants.' Her smile managed to hide the emotions seething behind it. 'Now, due to Gabriel, I know how to prune, and how to treat the grass, and which plants to put where when

I buy more. From now on I'll be able to cope alone.' In more ways than one, she thought savagely.

'You're lucky you found Gabriel there—he was supposed to be in Greece while Hector did the house-sitting for me. But Gabriel had a fight with his fiancée on holiday and decided to come home and vegetate for the rest of it, letting Hector off to dig up some field in Norfolk.'

Fiancée? thought Imogen wildly. 'This isn't Gabriel's home base, then?'

'Oh, no. He works in the City—lives near the job. I'm always telling him to get one of those nice little houses with a secluded garden in Westminster or somewhere, but he assures me that his lifestyle doesn't allow time for gardening. Pity, really. He's so good at it.'

He's good at a lot of things, thought Imogen bitterly. 'Do you have just the two sons, Mrs Sargent?'

'Two sons, one daughter. Kate's husband is in the diplomatic service. They're presently in Washington, which she likes very much, though personally I find the heat rather trying. Alice, my new granddaughter, is so adorable that it's a wrench to come away every time I visit.' Mrs Sargent accepted more coffee. 'It's excellent, my dear. Do you have any children?'

'Not of my own. Natasha, my stepdaughter, is eighteen, and fortunately we get on rather well. At the moment she's on holiday in France.' Imogen marvelled at how well she was carrying on the conversation, when all the time she wanted to hurl things round the room in a rage.

'I'm glad I stayed to chat,' said Mrs Sargent. She gave Imogen a searching look. 'I'm a widow myself, and at first I just wanted to shut myself up in the house and never talk to a soul. Of course that wasn't possible, with a family to think of, but I know the feeling. I'm glad you're past that stage.'

'It's almost a year now.' Imogen smiled bleakly. 'Time I got back to work. I'm applying for jobs.' She explained about her aim to find one in London that was sufficiently high-powered to allow her a modest flat of some kind and still to keep on the cottage.

'Must you work in London? Couldn't you find something in Cheltenham or Pennington and commute from here every day? It would save you the expense of another home. Even when you're not here you still have to heat the place and pay community tax and so on. A house eats money whether one inhabits it or not.'

Imogen's eyes narrowed. 'I hadn't really thought of that. I've only worked in London so I automatically thought I'd go back there. But if I can find work within driving distance of this place it's the obvious solution.'

'I was plainly meant to come here this morning,' said Mrs Sargent, getting up. 'I hope my suggestion will be useful.' She smiled. 'Come and see me. Any time. I can't promise such wonderful coffee but my door's always open. I'll give you a ring.'

Imogen thanked her unexpected visitor, saw her to the door, watching as Mrs Sargent paused for a chat with Gabriel on her way to the car. The moment her car was out of earshot Gabriel strode up the path to the kitchen door, kicked off his boots, and advanced towards her purposefully.

'Come to gloat?' she demanded.

'Imogen, listen—'

'No, *you* listen. You've had your joke, and a lot more besides,' she threw at him, 'but the game's over. You've made a complete fool of me, Gabriel *Sargent*, and now you can take your cheque and ride away into the sunset on your Harley-Davidson. Which, I take it, was just window-dressing. What do you really drive? An Aston Martin, or maybe something less chic, like a Porsche or—?'

'Stop it!' He took her by the shoulders, his fingers biting into her flesh. 'Imogen, I never meant to make a fool of you. But if you'd known I wasn't a bona fide gardener you wouldn't have let me work for you. And from the moment I saw you I wanted to do anything in the world I could for you—'

'Except tell me the truth.' She freed herself savagely.

'I meant to after the first day, but somehow it got out of hand.' He put out a hand, then dropped it as she backed away, her eyes blazing green fire at him. 'I was on the point of confessing several times at first. Then I realised you weren't totally indifferent to me and my baser side took over. Suddenly it was enormously important that you took me for what I am, not *who* I am.'

'In other words it was titillating to have Mrs Lambert falling for the lad who did her garden,' she said in disgust. 'Shades of Lady Chatterley!'

Gabriel's colour receded beneath his tan. *'Don't.'* He breathed in deeply. 'Imogen, locally people think you're very reserved. I knew that once you knew who I was you'd dispense with my services. And almost from the first I needed to see you every day—and more often than that when I could. The vegetables and books were just an excuse to come back in the eve-nings—'

'A clever variation on the usual flowers,' she said with sarcasm. 'It worked too. I was touched. So thoughtful, I said to myself. Yet in a village like this you were in danger of having your cover blown any time. I even came to the cricket match. Weren't you afraid someone would spill your secret by accident?'

'Not really. I was born here. Everyone knows me as Gabriel.' His mouth tightened and he looked away. 'At the match I was like a teenager showing off to his girl. I've been a fool.'

'And a liar.'

His head flew up, his eyes glittering dangerously. 'No. You can't lay that at my door. I've never lied. I just kept my surname a secret. I wasn't lying when I said everyone in the area calls me Gabriel.'

'I was bound to find out,' she said dully, suddenly sick of the entire conversation.

'At four this afternoon, to be precise,' he said quietly, his eyes locked with hers. 'I was going to make my grand confession, tell you that money wasn't necessary—'

'No, indeed,' she agreed, her mouth taut with dis-taste. 'You were paid in kind last night. Taking my money as well would have smacked of greed.'

He glared at her. 'For God's sake, Imogen, was that really necessary? I meant that I was glad to do the gardening for love.'

'Love!' She laughed scathingly. 'Talking of gar-dening, Gabriel Sargent, let's call a spade a spade. Love didn't enter into it. What we experienced together last night was a bit of good old-fashioned lust. You, I gather, had just broken up with the fiancée, and, on my part,' she added silkily, 'I'm a widow and it's a long time since there was any sex in my life. How could I refuse the attentions of a tasty young stud like you?' The moment the vulgar words were out of her mouth she would have given anything to take them back. The look in Gabriel's eyes cut like a surgeon's knife.

'After that there doesn't seem much to say,' he said, in a tone to match the icy revulsion in his eyes. 'I haven't quite finished everything I intended in your garden, but in the circumstances I'm sure you'll forgive me if I leave right now.'

'Of course,' she said with hauteur. 'I've made out the cheque, incidentally—I just need to fill in the name. It seemed unlikely that your bank would know you just as Gabriel.'

'Keep your money—or give it to charity,' he said through his teeth, and flung away through the door, sprinting down the path to the Harley-Davidson. He clapped the helmet on his shiny, dark head, kicked the engine into life, then roared off down the lane at a speed which set Imogen's teeth chattering with fear. She ran to the gate and waited, terrified, convinced he would crash. When nothing happened she went back into the house wearily, wishing she could put the clock back and start the day over again.

Hot tears dripped into the kitchen sink as she washed her Spode china. She dried it with care, wiping her eyes on the teatowel from time to time. Eventually there was nothing left to do—and the rest of the day to do it in.

She went upstairs and splashed her face with cold water, made it up more heavily than usual to hide the tear stains, then closed up the house and opened the garage. She was driven by a sudden deep need for the noise of a city. Gabriel had played his little joke, acted out his little charade, and now it was time to forget him. Less than two weeks ago, she reminded herself as she backed out into the lane, she hadn't known he existed.

She drove to Cheltenham as fast as the speed limit allowed, and as soon as she'd parked the car she took herself to a teashop to eat a sandwich and drink a pot of coffee to quell the terrible shaking feeling that Gabriel had left behind as his parting gift.

As she forced down a mouthful or two Imogen made herself take stock, put the entire acquaintance with Gabriel in perspective. His major sins from her point of view were of omission. What she really couldn't take was the fact that he had made love to her without telling her who he really was, and had come to her almost straight from the arms of the fiancée he'd neglected to mention. She thought of his laughter as they lay naked together and her stomach churned.

She pushed the remains of her sandwich aside, got up to pay the bill, then went out into the hot afternoon to buy up all the local papers she could find. Afterwards she bought a few things to eat, to save going into the village, then did some protracted window-shopping, hardly knowing what she looked at. In the end there was no alternative to going home, and she trudged wearily back to the car park and set off, cursing herself for dawdling when she realised that she was stuck in the middle of rush hour.

Imogen was so tired when she got home that at first she didn't see the envelope on the doormat. She put the food away, put the kettle on, found the 'Situations Vacant' pages of all the newspapers and spread them out on the kitchen table. It was only when she sat down to go through them that she saw the envelope lying there. She eyed it curiously, wondering if it was some kind of invitation. It had obviously come by hand. Her name was written in unfamiliar black handwriting, but with no address.

She slit the envelope open with a kitchen knife. Inside there was a photocopy of a birth certificate, which gave the date of birth of one John Gabriel Sargent, son of Claudia and Edward Sargent of Camden House, Abbots Munden. The date was less than a month later than her own. Give or take a week or two, Gabriel was the same age as herself.

John Gabriel Sargent was a fortunate man, she thought dully. Like Philip Lambert he looked years younger than his age. Quite a joke, really. A month could hardly be considered an age-gap. The barrier to their relationship now was his secrecy about his fiancée. Plus the unforgivable, scathing words she'd flung at him. As barriers went, she thought miserably, both were pretty insurmountable.

CHAPTER EIGHT

IMOGEN was no stranger to grief and loss. But after
the tragedy of Philip's death she'd been sure that
nothing would ever affect her so deeply again. It was
a blow to find that she was mistaken. The pain of
Gabriel's absence was unbearable. She kept glancing
through the kitchen window, as if by some miracle
she'd see the lean brown torso and gleaming dark head
as he worked in the garden.

She missed him with a physical ache, wishing bitterly that she'd never let him make love to her. Not
that there'd been much question of letting. They'd
both been helpless in the grip of an emotion that had
built between them, day by day, almost from the first
morning he arrived to work for her. But apart from
the heartache and the longing to have his arms round
her again she missed just chatting to him when she
took him coffee, missed the advice he gave her on
which plants thrived best in the soil at Beech Cottage.
Before Gabriel she'd looked on soil as just earth, not
something that differed according to location.

Determined to keep the garden in shape after he
had wrought such wonders with it, Imogen worked
in it diligently in an effort to channel her energies and
at the same time take the edge off the loneliness which
came back in full force now that she was alone again.

It helped when the builders returned the following
week to finish the boundary wall. They saw to their

own coffee-breaks, but Imogen enjoyed hearing their voices as they worked, even the pop music the youngest of them played on his transistor, after asking her permission.

She was surprised to receive a call from Mrs Sargent one day. They talked about the weather and the gardens for a while before Claudia came to the point.

'I wondered whether you'd done anything about job-hunting locally?' she asked.

Imogen explained that she'd bought papers in Cheltenham and applied for a few things which might be suitable. 'Unfortunately nearly all my experience has been in banking, Mrs Sargent, which narrows it down a bit.'

'Would you consider something as far afield as Pennington, Mrs Lambert?'

'Pennington. That's about eight miles or so from Gloucester, isn't it?'

'That's right. Fairly reasonable from here in commuting terms. I happened to be talking to an old beau of mine, Robert Hastings, the other night at a friend's dinner-table. He told me he's coming down to the Pennington branch of his bank to set up new overseas departments and so on. He's going to run the new operation himself until he retires next year.'

Imogen brightened. 'Does he need a PA?'

'Urgently, as it happens. The one he's got now flatly refuses to transfer from London, to his intense irritation. So I took it upon myself to mention your name.'

'That was very kind of you!'

'Nonsense. I like organising things. Interfering, Gabriel calls it.'

Imogen felt a sharp pang at the mere mention of
his name. 'I'm very grateful, Mrs Sargent. I'm a bit
out of practice at looking for work.'

'I'm sure you must be,' returned the other woman
with sympathy. There was a pause. 'Mrs
Lambert—'

'I'd be delighted if you'd call me Imogen.'

'Then I shall. And what I'm trying to say as tact-
fully as possible is that I'm worried that Gabriel might
have upset you in some way on Thursday. He was in
a filthy mood when he came home. He took off for
London almost at once, saying he had to settle in over
the weekend before going back to work. Which wasn't
his original plan at all.'

Imogen tried to think of something to say. 'I think
it was more the other way round, Mrs Sargent. I—I
think I offended him when it came to paying him for
the work he'd done.'

'Oh, *dear*! You offered him money?'

'I'm afraid so.'

'Didn't he make it clear that he was just helping
you out because Sam Harding was out of action?'

'Well, yes, in a way. But I would have paid Sam.'

'Not quite the same thing. Gabriel's the angel I
named him for in many ways, but if you hurt his pride
he can be an implacable devil.'

Imogen's heart sank. She couldn't even say that the
hurt had been unintentional. She'd spat her insult at
him, wanting to hit out at him in any way she could.
'I'm sorry I offended your son, Mrs Sargent. He did
a brilliant job on my garden, and I'm very grateful.'
Something suddenly occurred to her. 'Oh, by the way,
Mrs Sargent, Gabriel lent me some audio books of

yours, in case you've missed them. I'll return them
to you as soon as possible.'

'Keep them as long as you like—but don't wait until
then to come and see me. Why not pop round for tea
tomorrow? In the meantime I've got a number for
you to ring. If you're interested, Imogen, get on to
Robert's outfit straight away.'

'I will. Thank you.' Imogen scribbled down the details, accepted the invitation to tea with pleasure, then
rang off, feeling a lot better for having talked to
Gabriel's mother.

She dialled the Pennington number, gave a few details of her qualifications and experience, provided
her address and telephone number, and was promised
an application form by return of post. Afterwards she
contacted Dominic Harwood, the man who'd taken
over Philip's vice-presidency in London, and asked
him if he'd act as her referee.

'You're going back to work?' he said, surprised.
'We could always use someone of your experience
here, Imogen.'

She explained her circumstances, that it was only
practical to work somewhere within reach of Abbots
Munden, and Dominic, who had once been Philip's
protégé, assured her that he'd recommend her in
glowing terms to any prospective employer.

Next morning, instead of the expected application
form, she received a call from the bank in Pennington,
apologising for the short notice but asking if Mrs
Lambert could possibly come for an interview that
very morning. Imogen, astonished, was only too
pleased to drive there right away.

Dressed in a dark green suit of severe cut, an ivory silk blouse, no jewellery other than her watch and bracelet, she presented herself at the bank's chambers promptly on the stroke of noon. The new branch had taken over a listed George III building and renovated it with taste into very luxurious premises. Imogen was impressed. She handed over the CV she'd prepared, and sat down to a wait which was much shorter than expected before she was called in to see Robert Hastings.

He was a brisk, self-assured man of a type she knew only too well. He exuded energy and authority and made it plain that he was in Pennington to get this particular operation up and running and was in immediate need of someone with initiative and experience in the world of the merchant bank.

She had always enjoyed interviews, and answered his quick-fire questions with aplomb. His catechism was thorough, but Imogen was on familiar ground, knew her credentials were impeccable, and felt confident that she met with his requirements. The proposed salary, as expected, was less than that of her previous job, but it would do very comfortably to provide the upkeep of Beech Cottage—if she was offered the post.

Later that afternoon, her skirt replaced by her new trousers, the waistcoat worn loose over the ivory silk shirt, Imogen walked into Abbots Munden to take tea with Gabriel's mother. She carried a bag containing the Jane Austen and one of the thrillers that she'd already listened to, also a small box of expensive fondant creams, in the hope that Claudia Sargent had a sweet tooth.

The day was cooler than on her last visit. A breeze sent fat white clouds chasing across a blue sky above the venerable limestone roof tiles of the Sargent home. She turned in through open gates between drystone walls and walked under rustling trees sheltering a drive wide enough to accommodate the carriages that had once bowled along it up to the house. As she approached, the oak door opened wide and Claudia Sargent emerged, smiling.

'Hello, my dear; I was just arranging some roses in the parlour so I could keep a lookout for you. Come in, come in.'

Imogen followed her into a wide, panelled hall which felt cool after the sunshine outside. She handed her the audio books with thanks, then proffered the gift-wrapped box of fondants, feeling unaccustomedly shy.

'I hope you like these.'

'Imogen, how sweet of you—oh, dear, what a pun! Thank you so much; I adore sinful treats. Come into the parlour and sit down, and tell me how the job situation's progressing.'

Imogen gave an exclamation of pleasure as she took in the well-worn appeal of the room. Muted chintz hung at the small-paned windows and covered some of the furniture. Other chairs were of cushioned leather or faded brocade; books lined the alcoves on either side of the stone fireplace. A silver bowl of roses stood on a table near the window; watercolours of local Cotswold scenes hung in darker corners.

But Imogen's eyes were drawn involuntarily to three pencil drawings, grouped together. They were portraits—head and shoulders studies of two young men and a girl, all of them in their late teens. One of them was Gabriel, the other two obviously his brother and sister.

'You like those?' asked Mrs Sargent.

Imogen nodded, for the moment struck dumb by the sheer male beauty of Gabriel as a boy. 'They're quite wonderful.'

'Why, thank you!'

Imogen's eyes widened. 'You did them *yourself*?'

'I did indeed. And appreciate the unsolicited compliment.' She smiled, obviously pleased. 'All three were at the same stage when I did them—in the period between school and university. Kate first, then Gabriel, then Hector. Gabriel was the hardest to draw. He's a restless soul, finds it hard to sit still. But it came out quite well in the end.' She waved a hand to another drawing on the opposite wall. 'That's the latest. Miss Alice Beachamp, aged six months.'

The baby's head was truly exquisite, the curve of the cheek and the pouting bottom lip so perfectly executed that Imogen longed to trace it with her finger. 'She's a sweetheart!' she exclaimed. 'But how did you manage to keep her in one place?'

'With extraordinary difficulty and the aid of several photographs! Now let's have some tea. I'll just leave you for a moment to see to the kettle. Shan't be long.'

Alone, Imogen gazed her fill at Gabriel's youthful face, suddenly riven with pain. If only she could find some way of taking back the coarse gibe she'd flung at him. She shivered. She was in his home under false pretences. If his mother knew the truth of her relationship with Gabriel she'd probably send her visitor packing.

Mrs Sargent reappeared with a loaded tray and set it down on a table near the deep, chintz-covered chair that was obviously her own domain. Books were piled on the table beside it, a tapestry frame stood near by with a half-completed footstool cover stretched on it.

'I make rather a mess all round me,' said Mrs Sargent, pouring tea. 'But I see no point in clearing away the things I'm using. I never seemed to have much time to read, or sew, when Edward was alive. Now it's the way I fill my evenings. Especially in the winter when I can't get out in the garden. Did you find it hard to adapt when your husband died?'

'Yes. Very.' Imogen accepted a feather-light scone, generously buttered. 'Mmm, this is delicious. Baking's rather a new pastime to me. I never had time until I came here to live.'

'Why not?'

'I was my husband's personal assistant until he was forced to retire.'

'Forced?' said Mrs Sargent with interest.

'By a couple of strokes.'

'I see. Was he much older than you, then?'

'Twenty-five years.'

'And did the age-difference never matter?'

'Hardly ever.' Imogen smiled wryly. 'I'd find it harder to relate to a younger man.'

'Really?' Mrs Sargent shrugged. 'Edward was a few months younger than me, but we never gave it a thought.' Her face shadowed. 'I certainly never expected him to die before me. It sounds a terrible thing to say, but as you're a widow too I'll confide that at first I was angry with him. For dying. So silly, really.'

'But very natural. Until recently I felt the same.'

Shrewd grey eyes met moss-green ones with under-
standing. 'You must be very easy to talk to. I've never
told anyone about the anger bit before.' Claudia
Sargent breathed in deeply. 'Now, did you ring the
bank yesterday?'

'I did indeed!' Imogen went on to tell of the prompt
interview and her hopes that Mr Hastings might find
her suitable.

'I'm sure he will,' said Mrs Sargent, eyeing her
visitor in approval. 'You're a very good-looking girl,
Imogen, and if you worked for your husband until
he died I'm sure you must be a very efficient one.'

'Thank you for the "girl" bit,' chuckled Imogen.
'Actually, it was quite odd. All the other jobs remotely suitable for me seemed to want someone either
much younger or much older.'

'And how old are you?'

'Thirty-three in September.'

'Good heavens, are you really? You look a lot
younger. You're the same age as Gabriel, then. But
he was born in October.'

Imogen almost said, I know. 'He looks younger
than that too.'

'A gift, isn't it? Inherited from Edward, not me,
unfortunately. All three look years younger than their
age. Kate, needless to say, is very glad of it, but the
boys find it annoying on occasion. Gabriel's a workaholic because of it, but I suppose that has its plus
side. He wouldn't have climbed his particular ladder
so quickly if he hadn't worked his socks off to
counteract his air of youth.'

Longing to ask just exactly what Gabriel did in the
City, Imogen couldn't quite bring herself to put the

question, and after more tea, and a walk round the magnificent garden, she thanked Mrs Sargent and took her leave.

'Let me know how you get on,' ordered her hostess. 'I'm sure you'll get the job, but tell me anyway.'

'I will—either way,' she promised, and went home feeling happier than she'd done in days.

Just being in the house where Gabriel grew up had been an odd kind of comfort. It was a good thing, she thought wryly, that Mrs Sargent had no idea how close she'd come to losing the portrait of her elder son. Imogen had longed to seize it and carry it off home with her. Lovesick idiot! she thought scornfully. About time she pulled herself together and stopped languishing over someone who was quite obviously never going to want to see her again.

Tash rang that evening to ask cajolingly if she minded her staying on in France a bit longer. 'I'm having a great time, and Steph wants me to. Mrs Prescott told me to tell you she's delighted to have me stay until they all come home. I can travel with Chris then.'

Imogen smiled, enlightened. 'Of course you can stay, ninny! I'm fine. In fact I've been applying for jobs.'

'*Jobs*!' said Tash, thunderstruck. 'Why, are you bored, or—?' She paused. 'Imogen,' she went on in a small voice, 'didn't Daddy leave you any money? Do you have to work? You can have some of mine—'

'Darling, hush; that's not the reason. I can't just twiddle my thumbs at Beech Cottage for the rest of my life. I need occupation. I'm looking for work near enough to commute every day. I've worked for my living since I was twenty, remember. I'm not used to being a lady of leisure.'

'Are you telling me the truth?'

'Natasha Lambert, are you accusing me of lies? Seriously, love, I must do something. Even the garden's beaten into submission now.'

'Talking of which, has Gabriel left now?'

'Yes. Incidentally,' added Imogen, knowing Tash would find out sooner or later, 'I now know his other name. It's Sargent.'

'Sargent? Aren't those the people who live in that gorgeous old house near the church?'

'That's right. He's gone back to his job in London.'

'Really? What does he do?'

'Something in the City. Anyway, Mrs Sargent invited me to tea this afternoon.' Imogen went on to tell Tash about the interview and Mrs Sargent's help in making it possible. Shortly afterwards Tash's money ran out, and Imogen went upstairs to change into jeans and sweatshirt to do some weeding.

As she was putting her tools away a couple of hours later she heard the telephone ringing. Stripping off her gardening gloves, she raced up the path, tripped over a paving-stone and fell on her hands and knees. Cursing her clumsiness, she stumbled to her feet and arrived in the kitchen just as the phone stopped.

She glared at it malevolently. She hated not knowing who'd rung. At least it wasn't Tash. But it probably wasn't Gabriel either. And there was no one else she wanted to talk to, she thought with a sigh, and went off to have a bath.

Next morning she came downstairs early to the usual hubbub as the builders got into their stride with the almost completed wall. She picked up her post from the front door and went into the kitchen to make breakfast, her heart skipping a beat as she saw that one of the envelopes was from the Pennington bank. She tore it open to find that Robert Hastings was pleased to offer her the post of his personal assistant at the salary already mentioned, and would be glad if she would contact him as soon as possible to let him know when she could start. She gave a crow of delight and did a little war dance round the kitchen.

She rang the bank, arranged to start on Monday, then dialled Mrs Sargent's number, but there was no reply. She'd give her the glad news later, thought Imogen, and went upstairs to look through her wardrobe and decide which items needed laundering, ready to wear to work.

She kept herself occupied all day, putting the house in immaculate order and ironing several blouses to go with a couple of suits which would do very well for her role as Robert Hastings' assistant. She was putting them away when she heard a familiar roar, and her heart gave a sickening thud as a figure in helmet and leather jacket came through the gate on the familiar Harley-Davidson.

Gabriel looked taller than ever from her bedroom window, and she ran downstairs eagerly. Then he took off his helmet and revealed long black hair and aquiline features just like Gabriel's. Only it wasn't Gabriel.

'I'm Hector Sargent,' said her visitor with a friendly grin. 'Are you Mrs Lambert? If so you're a lot younger than I expected!'

She pulled herself together, finding it easy to smile at this engaging young replica of Gabriel. 'How do you do? And I really am Imogen Lambert. Won't you come in?'

'Thank you.' He sauntered into the kitchen, looking around him with interest.

'Would you like a drink?' she asked, waving him to a chair.

'I'd love a beer,' he said with regret, 'but my mother would make mincemeat of me if I went home on the bike smelling of best bitter. A coke would be nice,' he added hopefully.

Since this was Tash's favourite tipple Imogen had no trouble in granting his wish.

'Have you finished digging up antiquities in Norfolk?' she enquired.

'Mother told you about that?' His eyes kindled. 'It's back-breaking work but it's hellish exciting—especially when you turn up something really interesting like a coin or a shard of pottery.' He grinned apologetically. 'Sorry. I can bore for Britain when I get started. Ma tries her best not to nod off when I'm in full flow, but Gabe just tells me to shut up. Gabe's my brother.'

Imogen smiled noncommittally and waited, wondering why he'd come.

'Oh—sorry, I'm supposed to deliver an invitation.' He searched through numerous zipped pockets. 'Ah! Here it is.'

The invitation was one of Mrs Sargent's cards with 'Please join us for lunch on Sunday, 12.30' written by hand on the back.

'Ma said I wasn't to take no for an answer, and was there any news of the job.'

Imogen smiled jubilantly. 'Tell your mother I'd be delighted to come to lunch, and the news is good. I start on Monday.'

'Congratulations!' Hector raised his glass in a toast, drained it and got to his feet, towering over her. 'See you Sunday, then, Mrs Lambert.' He grinned engagingly. 'Do I have to call you that?'

'No. Imogen will do.'

'Good.'

'Thank you for coming in person with the invitation,' she said.

He gave her a rather wicked grin. 'It was my pleasure, Imogen. When Ma tells me to run errands, believe me, I do it. Forceful lady, my mother. But in this instance I was only too delighted. See you Sunday—if not before.'

She laughed, and waved as he straddled a long leg over the Harley. He waved back, put the helmet on and went off with a roar down the lane, looking so like Gabriel that Imogen spent a very restless evening.

One of her main problems was her sofa. It had always been her favourite place to curl up and read or watch television. Now it was the place where Gabriel had made love to her, and it would take a long, long time before she could even look at it without longing for the bliss she'd found in his arms. And would never find again.

CHAPTER NINE

IMOGEN drove to Camden House through a downpour to find that the Sargent invitation was to a party, not just a family lunch. Several cars were already parked in the drive, more along the lane outside. Glad that she'd chosen a dateless amber silk shift from her London life, she parked the car in the lane and put up an umbrella to shield the hair she'd taken so much trouble over.

At the door she was greeted exuberantly by Hector. His hair was caught back in a ponytail, but otherwise he'd bowed to convention—or his mother's decree— with a white shirt and immaculate chinos.

'Hi, Imogen—great dress! Come and meet everyone.' He led her across the hall to a large, formal drawing-room full of people and conversation. Claudia Sargent, crisp and uncluttered as usual in tailored blue linen, came hurrying to welcome the newcomer.

'Imogen, I'm so glad you could come! Let me introduce you to everyone.'

Imogen had no time to feel shy. Mrs Sargent's friends were welcoming, some people familiar by sight, others new to her, and suddenly it felt good to be chatting away in interesting company, a glass of wine in her hand. This was the type of occasion she'd enjoyed very much in the past. But she'd accepted no invitations at all since Philip died. This was her first real social event in Abbots Munden, and she relaxed, enjoying it all, until a familiar figure entered the room to give instructions to the young waiter serving drinks.

Her heart leapt under the silk, righting itself so abruptly that she felt dizzy and drank down her wine as if it were a dose of medicine. Then she noticed the girl following close behind Gabriel and burned with sudden, unadulterated jealousy. His companion was a tanned, beautiful blonde, with spectacular curves outlined by a pink thigh-length dress.

Imogen seethed. She had both hoped and dreaded that Gabriel would be here, but had never given a thought to the famous fiancée. And the tall, self-assured man threading his way through the guests, exchanging smiles and greetings as he came, was nothing like the Gabriel she knew.

Gone were the long, shaggy locks. His glossy hair had been sheared to lie just above his cream silk shirt collar, which was open at the neck of an unstructured, natural linen suit. And the girl with him was openly possessive, staying close by his side as she bestowed radiant smiles on everyone in her vicinity.

Halfway across the room Hector materialised to whisk the winsome blonde away, so Gabriel was alone when he finally reached Imogen. He greeted her formally, and exchanged a few pleasantries with her companions, who eventually excused themselves to go off and talk to friends.

He fixed her with a daunting grey eye. 'How are you?'

She smiled serenely. 'I'm very well. It was very kind of your mother to ask me here today.'

'I didn't know you'd been invited.'

'I didn't know you'd be here.'

They stared at each other, enclosed in a bubble of hostile silence among the convivial hubbub in the room.

Gabriel raised a black eyebrow. 'If you'd known would you have refused the invitation?'

'Yes,' she said, not altogether truthfully. She'd hoped quite desperately that he'd be here. But not with a clinging blonde fiancée in tow. And not with a new persona either. This self-contained, elegant man had nothing in common with the Gabriel who'd rushed to her in the storm and bowled her over with his tempestuous lovemaking.

'You mean you can't bear to be in my company?' he enquired tonelessly.

'Not at all. But I can't imagine that you yearn for mine.' She smiled brightly as Hector joined them.

'Briony insists on helping with lunch,' he announced, 'and Ma says it's my turn to do the congenial host bit. She asked you to keep Imogen entertained, Gabe; introduce her to anyone she doesn't know.' Hector's eyes sparkled wickedly as he sensed the tension in the air.

So her name's Briony, thought Imogen, smouldering.

'My pleasure,' said Gabriel smoothly.

'Thought it would be! Ma says lunch in ten minutes. Have a spot more bubbly, Imogen,' coaxed Hector as one of the waiters hovered.

She shook her head regretfully. 'I'm driving.'

'Go on,' he urged. 'You can always walk home.'

'True.' In desperate need of Dutch courage for once, she held out her glass for a refill. 'You've persuaded me.' She gave Gabriel a cold green glance. 'You don't have to, you know.'

'I don't have to what?'

'Stay here and entertain me. You must have others with more call on your time.'

'But none as gorgeous as you, Imogen!' Hector grinned, then sauntered off, leaving a tense silence behind him.

'I like your mother very much,' she said, to break it. 'She's very kind.'

'I did my damnedest to be kind too,' he said, looking away across the room.

'Oh, you were. But just a touch economical with the truth.'

'I didn't lie. I merely kept certain facts to myself.'

'Like your name, age and your way of earning your living!' she retorted. 'Not to mention your status!'

'You know my reasons. My age never had the least importance—but if I'd introduced myself as Gabriel Sargent you'd never have let me work for you.' He stopped suddenly. 'But this is all water under the bridge. You expressed your opinion of me in pretty memorable terms the day I left.' His mouth twisted in distaste.

She eyed him curiously. 'Why did you send me a copy of your birth certificate?'

'Who knows?' He shrugged impatiently. 'Bloody stupid thing to do, looking at it with hindsight. At the time I wasn't functioning normally.'

'I *am* older than you,' she remarked, doing her best to look as though their conversation were the usual inconsequential type that people indulged in at parties.

'What the hell difference does it make?' The demand was so quietly savage that the glass shook dangerously in her hand. 'You are you and I am me, whatever ages, names or any other blasted impediments you choose to dream up.'

'Ah, there you are, Gabriel,' said his mother, coming to interrupt. 'Thank you for looking after Imogen. Lunch is ready. Only a cold buffet,' she added. 'I counted on sunshine and lunch alfresco, but the wretched weather's let me down.' She shepherded Imogen across the hall to the dining-room, where a magnificent salmon lay in state on a bed of nasturtium blossoms as centrepiece of an impressive display.

To Imogen's relief Gabriel departed to welcome some latecomers, but Briony, she noted with venom, was serving out slices of game pie, very much daughter of the house. Speared by another dart of jealousy, she chatted to the others clustering round the table and helped herself sparingly to delicious food she didn't want. Gabriel and Briony, she thought grimly, made a very effective appetite depressant.

To Imogen's gratitude a friendly couple from Long Hinton invited her to sit with them on one of the cushioned window-seats looking out over the back garden, and she joined them, happy to listen to tales of their children's progress in school, and doing her best to pretend that Gabriel and Briony didn't exist.

'I'm to ask if you'd like seconds,' interrupted Hector before she'd managed to consume half her plate's contents. 'Come on, Imogen, you'll never be a big strong girl if you don't eat more.'

Apologetically she pleaded eyes out of step with her appetite, and Hector relented, taking her off to choose a dessert instead, telling her that his mother's strawberry cheesecake was an experience not to be missed.

'Did she do all this herself?' she asked in awe as she surveyed the various delectable desserts laid out on a side-table in the dining-room.

He leaned down confidentially to whisper in her ear, 'Mrs Jennings did the salmon, and quite a few of this lot, but don't tell Ma I let on.'

She giggled, then looked up in dismay to find Gabriel's eyes on them, ice-cold with disapproval.

'Get a move on, Hector,' he ordered. 'Collect plates, or round people up—'

'Or just get lost?' said Hector, grinning, then departed hurriedly at the look on his brother's face.

'I thought you weren't partial to *youthful* male company,' said Gabriel, his malevolent undertone at odds with the smile on his face.

Imogen looked down at the slice of cheesecake on her plate, wondering what on earth to do with it. 'Hector's your brother!' she muttered.

'What the hell has that got to do with it?' He raised his voice. 'If you're interested in nineteenth-century literature my father collected a few rare editions together,' he remarked, startling her considerably.

'That's right,' said his mother, looking up from the fruit terrine she was serving. 'I know you're a Jane Austen fan, Imogen, but Edward's collection of Victorian writers is well worth a look.'

Gabriel grasped Imogen's arm with a relentless hand, ignoring the fury on Briony's face, and, given no chance to protest, Imogen found herself in a book-lined room with the door shut and Gabriel standing against it. Suddenly, ludicrously, she realised that she still had the plate of cheesecake in her hand.

'I really can't eat this,' she said abruptly. 'Can you dispose of it so that your mother won't be hurt?'

He took it from her and dumped it on the desk. 'You care a damn sight more for other people's feelings than you do for mine.'

She had nothing to say to this. Gabriel Sargent in this mode was a stranger, she thought miserably, a far cry from the ragged young Adonis who'd done her gardening.

'We're supposed to be looking at books,' she reminded him at last.

'To hell with the books!' He moved closer. 'You know damn well I brought you in here to talk to you in private.'

Her eyes flashed coldly. 'I can't see why. Your fiancée didn't like it at all.'

His face darkened. 'Briony is not my fiancée any longer.'

'What difference does that make? She was! What did you think I meant by status—your social standing in the community?' she said bitingly. 'I didn't care a damn about that. Ever. I was referring to commitments. It came as something of a surprise when your mother mentioned your fiancée—just in passing, I hasten to add.'

'And what did she say?'

'That you'd gone on holiday to Greece together. I thought that tan of yours was a bit deep-dyed for a British sun!'

'The holiday was a mistake. I'd known for some time that things weren't working out between us, but Briony pleaded to keep to the original arrangements. I was bloody relieved when we met up with some friends of hers almost as soon as we arrived. They were on a yachting holiday.'

Gabriel shrugged. 'Briony decided the best way to revive my interest was to make me jealous. The wealthy, newly divorced owner of the boat was only too glad to oblige her and urged us to go island-hopping with the party. Briony promptly accepted, but I refused, only too glad to escape from a situation I'd begun to find intolerable. After floods of tears and acrimonious arguments she finally went off on the yacht. I spent a couple of days alone in the sun in peace, then got bored and came home.'

'And decided a little light entertainment with me would compensate for what you'd been deprived of in Greece,' said Imogen coldly. 'I suppose it amused you to see how quickly the gardener could make it to the lonely, sex-starved widow's bed.'

His eyes blazed with distaste. 'If that's the construction you put on what happened between us there's nothing more to be said.' He strode to the window and stood with his back to her. 'Have you done anything about a job?'

'Yes,' she said, startled by the abrupt change of subject. 'Your mother hasn't mentioned it?'

'No. You are not a subject I find easy to discuss. With anyone.'

She pulled herself together. 'Your mother gave my name to a friend of hers, Robert Hastings. She heard he was looking for a PA and thought I might fancy working in Pennington. I was lucky. I got the job.'

He turned to look at her. 'You've changed your mind about working in London, then?'

'For the time being, yes.' She glanced at her watch. 'I must be going. I start work tomorrow. I've things to do.'

'It's only just after four. Your preparations won't take that long, surely?'

'No. But it never does to outstay one's welcome,' she said evenly.

'Don't I know it!' he retorted bitterly, and opened the door for her.

'Will it be all right for me to leave my car out in the lane?' she asked as they rejoined the party.

'I've had very little to drink—I'll drive you home,' he said swiftly.

'And infuriate Briony even more?' She shook her head. 'I think not. Thank you just the same. I'll just say goodbye to your mother and Hector.'

'Briony,' he said with controlled violence, 'is not here by invitation—mine or my mother's. She just took it into her head to drive down from London this morning—"to mend fences", as she put it. I made it plain that I wasn't interested, but as she'd driven from town my mother felt duty-bound to ask her to stay for lunch. End of story.'

'Ah, but is the story fact or fiction?' she asked lightly. 'Either way it's nothing to do with me.'

He stood by in stony silence as she thanked Claudia Sargent and exchanged a few words with Hector, who watched, openly curious, as she turned to Gabriel. 'I forgot to mention that your mother's persuaded Sam

Harding to spare a few hours a week for my garden. You did such a splendid job it won't be difficult to tame from now on. Thank you for showing me your father's book collection. Goodbye.'

Gabriel just stood there, powerless to force his company on her as she reiterated her thanks, assured her hostess that a walk would be pleasant now that the rain had stopped, and, with an all-encompassing smile to the three Sargents, walked without haste down the drive and out of Gabriel's life.

Imogen was grateful for the demands of the new job. It channelled all her energies so thoroughly that she fell into bed every night during the first week too tired to think of Gabriel for more than the few minutes it took her to get to sleep.

Robert Hastings was a man who worked hard and expected his staff to do the same, but Imogen, accustomed to men of his calibre, had no quarrel with that. Her job with Philip had been equally demanding, if not more so. After the first day or two of finding her bearings she began to enjoy the work, glad to feel part of a world which stretched beyond the boundaries of Beech Cottage and out into the world of international banking and finance that she'd once known so well.

Mr Hastings made it plain from the beginning that his reign at Pennington would finish when he retired a year later.

'Of course, Mrs Lambert, if you wish to continue I'm sure my replacement would be grateful for an assistant of your experience and flair.' He smiled, his eyes twinkling. 'I know it's a little premature to forecast a faultless working relationship, but I think you'll agree that you and I deal well together.'

'I do indeed, Mr Hastings,' she returned, secretly very pleased. After the break away from her career she'd had a certain amount of misgiving about returning to the fray. Yet now, after only a short time back in harness, she couldn't imagine how she'd endured the long days alone at Beech Cottage.

When Tash rang from France a week or so later Imogen gave her all the details of the new job, convincing her stepdaughter that she was really enjoying the work and not dragging herself to Pennington every day merely to earn the money.

'Definitely not, love,' she said firmly. 'Now that I'm back in the swim again I can't imagine how I managed to vegetate at the cottage so long. But I'm sorry, Tash, I'm afraid I'll be pretty tied up during the week when you come back. Would you prefer to stay with Barbara and Henry?'

'I'll swap around a bit—weekends with you, weekdays with Gran and—' Tash hesitated. 'Perhaps I could have Steph to stay at the cottage for a bit—sort of a return for my holiday?'

Imogen assured her that she could invite any of her friends, as long as they did their own catering. 'I'll provide the food, Tash, but you'll have to cook it. I'm pretty done in by the time I get home.'

Tash promised that Imogen wouldn't need to lift a finger, said she'd be home some time the following Saturday evening, then gave stern instructions to her young stepmother not to wear herself out and said goodbye, with her usual affectionate kisses blown down the line.

Imogen rang Claudia Sargent once she'd established her working routine, with sincere thanks for her part in getting her the new job.

'I merely mentioned your name, my dear! You did the rest. Robert's a good friend, but he wouldn't have engaged you on my recommendation if you weren't up to scratch.'

Imogen, pleased, promised to report again in due course. Mrs Sargent, however, rang back instead a couple of days later to enquire for herself. Imogen was able to assure her that things were going well, that she enjoyed working in Pennington, and had no rapport problems with her employer.

'I'm glad,' said Claudia Sargent with satisfaction. 'I wish I could say the same regarding my sons. Hector is finding the summer vacation boring now that the dig is temporarily suspended in Norfolk. Digging the garden instead holds no charm for him. And Gabriel, during the brief minute he spares me on the phone, is obviously not pleased with life.

'I suppose the break-up with Briony's to blame. I thought they might have patched things up when she came running down here the day of the lunch, but apparently not. Gabriel can be an unforgiving soul.'

Imogen's involuntary chill melted in a surge of elation. Gabriel had been telling the truth. The engagement had not been resumed after all.

She arrived home on the third Friday evening of her new working life to a feeling of anticipation. Tash was coming home.

The garden was looking quite glorious, owing to Sam Harding's expertise, added to her own weekend diligence. With no weeding to do for once, she spent the evening preparing food for the next day. As she was clearing up the telephone rang. She picked it up, frowning, hoping it wasn't Tash with a change of plan, and almost dropped it when she heard Gabriel's voice.

'Imogen? I'm in luck this time. At Mother's lunch I forgot to mention that there was no answer when I rang before. How are you?'

So her caller had been Gabriel. 'Very well,' she said brightly. 'And you?'

'Couldn't be better. I thought I'd ask how the job was going. Mother said you got off to a good start with Robert Hastings.'

'I did. I like him—and it's exactly the type of work I'm used to.'

'Glad to hear it.' He paused. 'Imogen, I'm coming down to Abbots Munden in the morning. Will you have dinner with me tomorrow evening?'

Imogen sat down suddenly. 'Sorry. I can't.'

There was a pause. 'I see. I suppose it was too much to hope that you'd be free at such short notice. Sunday, then?'

'I'm afraid not.'

'*Why* not?' he demanded with sudden urgency. 'I've been bloody patient, giving you time to cool down. Stop playing games, Imogen!'

'You were the one playing games,' she said furiously. 'Your ego took a beating in Greece, and the episode with me restored it. "End", I quote, "of story". Goodbye, Gabriel.'

'Don't hang up!' he ordered harshly. 'Let's get one thing clear. If I set out to seduce a woman, Imogen,

I sure as hell don't slog for hours in her garden as foreplay!'

And to Imogen's rage he slammed the phone down, denying her the satisfaction of beating him to it.

CHAPTER TEN

TASH arrived home looking brown and flaxen-fair from the sun, and laden with gifts. She showered Imogen with duty-free Eau de Givenchy, a bottle of Dom Pérignon, an earthenware dish of a pâté recommended by Mrs Prescott, and an exquisite Limoges porcelain plate to hang on the wall.

'Limoges was the nearest big town,' said Tash when they were sitting down to supper. Chris Prescott had driven her home, and had quite obviously wanted to stay, but Tash had seen him firmly on his way with no more than coffee and cake.

'Chris could have stayed to supper, you know,' Imogen said.

'No. I wanted you all to myself.' Tash smiled demurely. 'Anyway, he's coming back when he brings Steph over to stay.'

'I see!' Imogen chuckled. 'I take it he's smitten.'

'A bit.'

'Are you?'

Tash grinned noncommittally. 'Never mind all that. How's the job?'

The evening passed swiftly as Tash talked nineteen to the dozen about her holiday and bombarded Imogen with questions, some of them about Gabriel.

'He's back in his alter ego role, doing something in the City,' said Imogen.

'Now that you're chums with Mrs Sargent haven't you asked exactly what?' her stepdaughter demanded.

'No. The subject never came up.' She gave a brief report on her lunch at Camden House, then changed the subject to France, and Tash was off again, only too happy to describe the glories of summer in the Périgord.

Next morning Imogen found that she was short of milk. 'I forgot to buy cream for the strawberries too,' she said, annoyed.

'Never mind. I'll take a hike down to the village stores. They open for an hour or so on Sunday, don't they?'

'I think so. Since I started work I'm afraid I haven't patronised the local shop as much as I should. If you are going I'll give you a list, Tash. Explain to Mrs Jennings why I haven't been in recently, would you?'

Tash went off happily while Imogen went back to the kitchen to check on the roast she never bothered with on her own. She finished preparing vegetables and took a look through the Sunday papers, until eventually it dawned on her that Tash was taking rather a long time.

She went out into the garden at last for a look down the lane, but no suntanned little figure in jeans and vest-top was in sight. She turned back into the garden, wondering if she should get the car out, when the familiar roar of a motorcycle shattered the Sunday morning peace, and the Harley-Davidson turned into the gate, ridden by a lanky, helmeted figure, with a small, helmeted passenger riding pillion.

'Hi, Imogen,' greeted Hector, removing his helmet. He lifted Tash off the bike. 'I gave Tash a lift home.'

'So I see. Hello, Hector,' said Imogen, annoyed to find herself affected by the mere sight of the Harley. 'I was wondering where she was.'

'Sorry, Imogen,' said Tash, her eyes sparkling as she handed her a carrier bag. 'But I ran into Gabriel coming out of the shop and he introduced me to Hector, and Hector offered me a ride. It was absolutely *brilliant*—and guess what? There's another cricket match this afternoon!'

'Will you come and watch, Imogen?' asked Hector eagerly. 'Tash said you witnessed Gabe's last triumph—and today you get two Sargents for the price of one.'

'I thought your game was rugby,' said Imogen.

'How did you know that?' he asked, astonished.

'Your brother borrowed your shirt to do Imogen's gardening,' Tash said, grinning.

'Ah, yes,' said Hector, gazing around at the now immaculate garden. 'I'd forgotten that. It's hell having a brother like Gabriel. He's such a class act.'

'Can you bat like him? That's the question!' teased Tash, obviously very comfortable already in his company.

'Gabe's an Oxford cricket blue,' he said ruefully. 'I'm not in the same class.'

'Perhaps he was a duffer at rugby,' consoled Tash.

'He's not a duffer at anything,' Hector returned, depressed, then brightened. 'Anyway, ladies, promise you'll come this afternoon. Support like yours could make all the difference between victory and defeat!'

Imogen laughed. 'I find that hard to believe. But I brought some work home with me, I'm afraid. I must get it done to take back tomorrow. But you go, Tash, by all means.'

'On my own?' said Tash, dismayed.

'If Imogen's busy I'll come and fetch you,' Hector said promptly. 'I'll probably be out first bat, so I can keep you company while Gabe makes the inevitable century.'

Over lunch, which Imogen brought forward hastily so that Tash could be ready for the match, there was much argument on the subject of Imogen's working too hard.

'You'll be nose to the grindstone all week,' complained Tash. 'Couldn't you come out this afternoon and enjoy some fresh air?'

'Sorry. If I do I'll have to work this evening.'

Imogen would have liked nothing better than to watch cricket on a sunny afternoon, just as before, but to turn up would convince Gabriel that she'd thawed. Which she hadn't, because, after accusing him of using her as a substitute for Briony, she now felt convinced that this had been the exact truth. At least to start with. And the very thought of it was like fire on her skin.

Hector duly arrived on his gleaming steed, and Tash, the helmet incongruous with her flowered cotton trousers and scoop-necked T-shirt, went off with him, after one last bid to change Imogen's mind.

'Can I take her for a drink at the pub afterwards?' asked Hector as he slung a long leg over the bike.

'Ask Tash, not me!' said Imogen, and waved them off with her blessing.

Having said she must, she made herself work solidly for a while, polishing up a report she'd prepared in draft form. Eventually she closed her laptop computer and decided to take a breather in the shape of a long, relaxing bath.

She lay in warm, scented water, wondering if Gabriel was murdering the visiting team's bowling as he'd done before. She would have loved to watch but hurt pride kept her from accepting the olive branch he'd offered. According to his mother, there had always been girls in his life, swarming, it seemed, like bees round a honey pot. And Imogen Lambert had no intention of being one of a number, no matter how much she wanted him.

And she did want him. She closed her eyes in sudden, searing self-knowledge. She was in love with him in a way she'd never been with Philip, or anyone else.

Cold water in full flood over the head did wonders for one's common sense, Imogen discovered, gasping. Half an hour later she was back at the kitchen table with her laptop, hair shining, her cotton dress cool in the summer sunlight which streamed in behind her from the open door. She forced herself to concentrate, intent on finishing before Tash came home.

In her absorption she didn't see the approaching shadow or hear the silent footfalls behind her. Her sudden, involuntary scream died at birth, smothered by a hard, familiar mouth as Gabriel pulled her from her chair into arms which closed round her like a vice and kissed her until her lungs were bursting.

He lifted his head at last and glared into her outraged eyes. 'Why didn't you come?'

'I didn't want to!' she spat.

'Liar!' he snarled, and bent his head to hers, but this time she was ready for him and twisted away, her colour high as her eyes flashed fire.

'What do you think you're doing? I'm not some compliant, sex-starved idiot you can make use of any time you're down in Abbots Munden with time on your hands.'

'You know bloody well I don't think of you like that!' he cut back with equal violence. 'When I ran into Tash I realised why you were tied up this weekend. You deliberately let me think some man was monopolising your time. I was angry.'

She raised a scornful eyebrow. 'Why? How I spend my time, and with whom, is nothing to do with you.'

'I happen to think it is.' He stood, arms folded, a green grass stain on one knee of his white trousers, the sleeves of his cricket shirt rolled to the elbows and his striking, suntanned face full of an arrogance so much at odds with the Gabriel of their early acquaintance that her secret little flame of resentment flared higher even as her pulse raced madly at the mere sight of him.

'Then you're wrong,' she informed him, calmer now. 'Whatever there was between us is over.'

'I refuse to accept that.' He thrust a hand through his hair with sudden impatience. 'There's no reason for it to be over.'

'Other than my wishes,' she said flatly, and saw his colour rise ominously under the tan.

'We found something rare together,' he said urgently. 'And I don't mean just the sex, blast it. Imogen, are you going to deny the rapport we felt from the first? I know you couldn't cope with that originally because I was the hired help and you were the widowed lady of the house, quite apart from all the other baggage you seemed to carry around with you as objections. But later you surrendered to it. Admit it.'

She nodded coolly. 'I was lonely and had too little to do with my time. Neither of those things applies any longer. And don't try to tell me that Briony, or someone like her, isn't waiting for you in London, panting to provide consolation.'

'There's no one,' he said savagely. 'Since that night—' He stopped dead, turning away. 'I don't *want* any other woman. Damn funny, isn't it?'

'Not really. Just *very* hard to believe.'

He leapt towards her then stopped in his tracks, cursing, as the Harley roared in through the gate. Imogen's heart sank as Tash came running in, followed closely by Hector.

'Hi, Gabriel,' Tash said in surprise.

'I thought you were walking home,' said Hector with a sweetly innocent smile. 'Took the scenic route, Gabe?'

'I wanted a word with Mrs Lambert,' said his brother curtly. 'Unfortunately I interrupted her at her computer.'

'Haven't you finished *yet*, Imogen?' asked Tash indignantly.

'I have, actually. At least, enough to make life easier at work tomorrow.' She smiled brightly. 'Can I offer anyone a drink?'

Hector accepted with enthusiasm. 'I only had one glass of shandy at the pub. Just let me drink a Coke, Gabe, and I'll run you back on the bike.'

'Please stay,' urged Tash. 'You've got to celebrate Hector's day of glory.'

Imogen went to the refrigerator for two cans of Coke, and, without thinking, automatically snapped open a can of beer and poured it into a glass tankard for Gabriel. 'I forgot to ask,' she said. 'Victory was yours again, I take it?'

Gabriel accepted the beer as automatically as Imogen provided it, much to the interest of the younger pair. 'Not mine, Hector's,' he told her. 'I, alas, failed to score today.' He gave her a look over the tankard, bringing colour to her face.

'Oh, bad luck,' she said brightly. 'So did you do better, Hector?'

He nodded jubilantly. 'I made thirty-four runs— never scored more than twenty before in my life!'

'You could hardly fail to with that redhead in the shorts cheering you on,' said Tash, grinning.

'Debbie from the Dog and Trumpet,' said Hector smugly.

Imogen laughed. 'Sorry I missed all the excitement.'

He threw his brother a sly look. 'You could have kept Gabe company while the rest of us did our bit for the glory of Abbots Munden.'

'Don't rub it in,' said Gabriel ruefully, and, to Imogen's dismay, settled himself in a chair at the kitchen table.

'Why don't you both stay for supper?' said Tash eagerly, turning appealing eyes on Imogen. 'That's OK by you, love, isn't it?'

Her heart sank. 'Of course,' she said brightly, avoiding Gabriel's eyes. 'Only salad and cold cuts, I'm afraid—'

'Perfect,' said Hector with relish, and eyed his brother. 'You weren't driving back to town tonight, were you, Gabe?'

'No.' Gabriel gave Imogen a challenging smile. 'I'd be delighted to stay to supper.'

'Great!' said Tash, and jumped to her feet. 'Right, then, Hector. You and I are the drones in this company, so we get the supper and let the two worker bees relax in the sitting-room with G and Ts until it's ready.' She gave Gabriel a grin. 'You can imbibe quite happily if Hector's doing the driving!'

'It had occurred to me,' he admitted, 'but if supplies allow I'll keep to beer.' He gave Imogen a steady look. 'If I mix my drinks I might get out of hand.'

Hector hooted. 'That'll be the day. Right, then, Miss Tash, just let me make a quick call to Ma to explain, then I'm all yours.'

A few minutes later, banished from the kitchen by Tash, Imogen found herself alone in the sitting-room with Gabriel, quite the last occurrence she'd expected to round off her Sunday.

'Do you mind?' he asked, standing in front of the fireplace.

She curled up in the corner of the sofa, her long skirt furled around her. 'I could hardly object. Tash obviously welcomed the company and—'

'My little brother was in complete agreement.' He smiled wryly. 'His adrenalin's still flowing—and long and lanky he may be, but he's only twenty. Just like you I hadn't the heart to put a damper on his pleasure.'

She looked down into the glass of mineral water she was holding, a wry twist to her mouth.

'Why the Mona Lisa smile?' asked Gabriel softly.

She shrugged, and raised her head to look him in the eye. 'It just occurred to me that we're having dinner together after all.'

'Just as I wanted,' he agreed, a disquieting light in his half-veiled eyes. 'Well—not entirely as I wanted. A dinner *à deux* was my intention, but this is better than not seeing you at all.'

'Why *did* you want to see me?'

'I would have thought that was perfectly obvious,' he said, in a tone which flipped her heart in her chest. 'I want you, Imogen. You know that. Since that night I haven't been able to get you out of my mind.'

She kept her voice steady with effort. 'Is this the chat-up line you take with all women, Gabriel? It's a bit direct.'

'There haven't *been* that many women, contrary to what you've heard.' He stared down at her broodingly. 'Besides, the others were just girls—'

'Thanks,' she said bitterly.

'Don't be stupid! I don't care a damn how old you are.'

'Just how old do you think I *am*?' she demanded hotly.

He grinned disarmingly, looking suddenly like the youth that she'd believed him to be. 'I've no idea, and have no intention of guessing either. All I know is that you're older than me, though Lord knows that's hard to believe. Sitting curled up like that, with the sun full on your face, you look very little older than Tash.'

'I'm fifteen years older than Tash,' she said flatly.

His slanting black brows drew together. 'Which makes you—'

'Thirty-three in September.'

He gave a bark of incredulous laughter. 'You mean you're literally one whole month older than me? Dear me, Mrs Lambert, what a decrepit old lady you are, to be sure!'

'What's the joke?' demanded Tash, hurrying in.

'We were discussing age-gaps,' Gabriel informed her, and met Imogen's eyes. 'Or, to be more accurate, the lack of them.'

Tash looked from one to the other uncertainly. 'Well, could you stop the discussion now? Supper's ready and we're starving.'

'Hector's always starving,' said Gabriel, helping Imogen to her feet.

'So am I!' Tash giggled and rushed ahead to usher them into the dining-room, where she'd laid the table with a white linen cloth and made a hasty centrepiece of flowers from the garden to add a festive note. The simple meal consisted of a huge bowl of green salad, a dish of ripe tomatoes, the French pâté, a platter of cheese and another of sliced roast beef left over from lunch, embellished with devilled eggs.

'I did those,' said Hector proudly.

Gabriel stared at his brother in mock awe. 'Is there no end to your talents, my child?'

'I carved the beef too,' confided Hector smugly, 'but Tash did the rest.'

Imogen gazed, touched, at the hastily prepared feast. 'It all looks very good to me. Thank you, my children.'

The evening, which Imogen had approached with such reluctance at first, developed into one of the most entertaining she'd ever spent. By tacit agreement she established a temporary truce with Gabriel, a gesture he responded to in kind, playing his part as a dinner guest with such charm and ease that she found it easy to imagine his popularity on the dinner-party circuit in his own circle.

He paid Imogen and Tash equal attention, encouraged Hector to describe his finds at the Norfolk dig, and in turn made his young brother blush furiously by relating anecdotes of Hector's devilry as a child.

'You've left out the bit about dogging your footsteps when you brought your girlfriends home,' said Hector in retaliation. He grinned evilly. 'Ma never had to worry that you were getting up to any hankypanky—I stuck to you like glue. The perfect chaperon.'

'I never indulged in any hanky-panky,' retorted Gabriel, ignoring the general laughter. 'At least,' he added, eyes dancing, 'not at home anywhere near Ma's eagle eye.'

'I'm not surprised,' said Hector with feeling. 'Ma knows perfectly well how the human race perpetuates itself—and how much it likes doing it—but she doesn't expect any perpetuating under her roof until one is legally shackled. Remember the performance when Kate was engaged to Sam? They were living together in London, but at home Kate had to sleep in her own little bed and Sam was exiled to a guest-room.'

'No corridor-creeping at night?' Tash giggled.

'Not in our house,' said Hector, guffawing. 'The floorboards go off like gunshots if you set foot outside your door.'

Imogen joined in the general laughter, but her colour rose as she met Gabriel's eyes across the table. The sudden leap of heat in them told her very plainly that he wanted to make love to her right that minute and she looked away swiftly, jumping up to collect plates with unsteady hands.

'I'm afraid all I can offer by way of a pudding is a slice of cake or your choice from that bowl of fruit over there.'

No one, it seemed, could eat another thing.

'But I'd very much appreciate some of that coffee of yours, Imogen,' said Gabriel.

'You make the coffee, then, Imogen,' said Tash. 'Come on, Hector. We'll clear up.'

The coffee was ready long before Tash and Hector had finished their labours. Gabriel took the coffee-tray from Imogen and followed her to the sitting-room.

'Thank you,' he said quietly as he set it down on the table beside her.

'What for?' she asked, her hand steady as she poured.

'For the evening. For giving Hector the opportunity to celebrate with Tash. For your magnanimity.'

'That's a long word.' She handed him a cup. 'You mean my manners were good enough to pretend that you and I were—friends.'

He leaned back in one of the deep chairs, his eyes holding hers. 'Must there be pretence? Why can't we be friends, Imogen?'

'Is that what you want?' she asked quietly.

'No,' he said bluntly. 'No more subterfuge, Imogen. I want to be your lover.' He leaned forward with sudden urgency. 'I already feel that I am your lover, that what we shared that night was too perfect to be just a passing fling, that you must have felt something for me to give yourself to me. No matter what insults you flung at me on the subject afterwards,' he added bitterly.

She gazed at him in silence, feeling herself melt towards him. 'Gabriel—' She paused, unable to put what she wanted to say into words.

'You're thawing!' he said in triumph, the light in his eyes so brilliant that she felt dazzled. 'No—don't back off. I don't expect miracles—not at first, but—'

'Imogen!' said Tash, rushing into the room. 'Guess what Hector just told me!'

'Is it something fit for us grown-ups to hear?' said Gabriel drily, sitting back in his chair.

'Tash asked where you worked, that's all,' said Hector, looking very sorry that he'd said a word.

Imogen's eyes narrowed in surprise at the glare Gabriel gave his brother. 'Is it a secret, then?' she asked lightly. 'Are you a double agent, or an inspector of taxes—?'

'I work in a bank,' he said briefly, his jaw tightening as she stared at him with blatant curiosity.

'What bank?'

'The same one you work for!' Tash beamed. 'Isn't that a coincidence? Apparently this Mr Hastings of yours used to be Gabriel's boss.'

The look that Imogen turned on Gabriel was as cold and green as ice over moss, all trace of a thaw vanished. 'Odd you never thought to mention it.'

'Oh, Lord,' said Hector in misery. 'I've obviously put my foot in it.'

Imogen gave him a brilliant smile. 'Not at all, Hector. In fact you've done me a favour.'

Tash, looking very subdued, took Imogen's hand. 'I shouldn't have been so nosy.'

'It's not a state secret,' said Gabriel, and got up. 'I was going to tell you, Imogen, but up to now the right moment hasn't presented itself.'

'Strange,' she retorted. 'You knew about my background in banking—and that I got the job in the Pennington branch; I would have thought that the right moment would have popped up more than once. I assume you know Mr Hastings well?'

Gabriel shrugged. 'His wife doesn't invite me to dinner, if that's what you mean. I'm a good few rungs below him on the ladder. I run the trading floor in the City; he's just given up the vice-presidency to take it easy in the Pennington branch until he retires. And my mother went to school with his wife,' he added.

Imogen felt Tash's hand tighten, and she smiled down at her in reassurance.

'Don't look so worried, Tash,' said Gabriel, his eyes softening. 'I'm to blame, not you.'

'Tash!' said Hector urgently. 'Walk down the garden with me.'

Tash went hastily, and in the silence left by their departure Imogen gave Gabriel a hostile little smile.

' "No more subterfuge", you said,' she reminded him. 'Not quite true, was it?'

'It didn't seem important,' he said curtly.

'Well, it is really,' she said, as though explaining something difficult. 'You see, Gabriel, it makes me wonder how many more facets of your personality still lie hidden.'

He moved suddenly, seizing her hands. 'None. That's it. Everything. What you see is what you get.'

'Always supposing that what I see I want,' she said cruelly.

He dropped her hands and stepped back. 'True.' His face hardened to a handsome, sculpted mask. 'All right, Imogen, I give up. For now. I meant what I said about wanting to be your lover but this isn't the time to press the point, with Hector waiting at the gate and a start at daybreak for me in the morning. Time, tide and corporate finance wait for no man—but I don't have to tell *you* that, Mrs Lambert.'

'No,' she agreed coolly. 'I've been through all that once.'

'You wouldn't have to go *through* anything with me, Imogen,' he said with urgency. 'I don't want you to work for me. I want you to live with me, share the life that I keep separate from takeovers and mergers. I want—'

'Let's talk about what *I* want,' she interrupted. 'If I were in the market for a lover, companion—call it what you like—I'd prefer a man who told me what and who he was from the first moment I met him. Peeling the layers of mystery away makes me uneasy as to how many other layers are left that I don't know about. But all that's academic anyway because I prefer my life the way it is. Without a man in it.'

'You're lying!' The arrogant confidence in his smile set her teeth on edge. 'You can say what you like, Imogen. It won't make any difference. I'm going to change your mind sooner or later.' The pupils of his eyes darkened hypnotically until they glittered like jet. 'My preference is sooner, but if it's later then I'll wait with what patience I can until you give in.'

'And if I don't?' she said unevenly, ensnared by the gaze locked with hers.

'You will!' He caught her in his arms, kissing her with an emphasis designed to convince.

'Oh, hell—sorry!' said a stifled voice and they sprang apart, Imogen's face blazing as she saw Tash and Hector hovering, embarrassed, in the doorway.

Gabriel raised a wry eyebrow. 'As must be perfectly obvious, not nearly as sorry as I am.' There was a flagrantly triumphant gleam in his eyes as he said goodnight to Imogen. 'Thank you for supper and a delightful evening. You'll be hearing from me,' he added deliberately, then said goodnight to Tash and bore his young brother off into the warm starry night.

'Gosh,' said Tash with contrition. 'I'm really sorry, Imogen. I mean, we wouldn't have come back, only Hector knew Gabriel's off at half o'clock in the morning back to London—'

'Don't apologise,' said Imogen, with a sudden, exhausted yawn. 'It was only a goodnight kiss.'

'If you say so!' Tash gave her stepmother a wicked smile. 'From where I was standing it looked as if perhaps it was a good thing we *did* interrupt!'

Perhaps it was, thought Imogen as she got ready for bed. In future she would keep Gabriel Sargent at arm's length. One touch was like a match to a powder keg whenever they were together. It had never been that way with any other man. Marriage with Philip had been a combination of shared interests as well as the sexual attraction that she'd known perfectly well she possessed for him.

She frowned as she turned out the light. And that, of course, was the whole crux of the matter. She had certainly found Philip attractive, but it had always been he who instigated their lovemaking. With Gabriel it was different. One touch of his mouth and hands and both of them went up in flames together. And that, she decided firmly, was no basis for a long-term relationship—too hot not to cool down. Because when it did cool down . . . what then?

CHAPTER ELEVEN

'MR HASTINGS,' said Imogen, just before lunch the next day, 'how well did you know Gabriel Sargent when you were in the City?'

Robert Hastings, a large, impressive man with a shock of iron-grey hair, looked across his desk, frowning. 'Young Sargent? Reasonably well. Why?'

She looked noncommittal. 'I only recently discovered what he does for a living.'

Her employer looked blank. 'Didn't he tell you that he runs the trading floor in London?'

'No.'

'Hmm. Odd. Know him well, do you?'

'Not very. And not nearly as well as I thought,' she said, unable to control the acid in her voice.

Mr Hastings grinned. 'Actually he's a very able chap, young Gabriel. Some say brilliant. Probably get my job by the time he's forty.' He eyed the composed young woman sitting opposite him. 'I must have got the wrong end of the stick. Claudia said he was a particular friend of yours.'

'Mrs Sargent?' Her eyes widened. 'Are you sure she meant me?'

'I may be in line for retirement but I'm not in my dotage yet,' he said with asperity. 'Claudia told me that her son knew a Mrs Imogen Lambert who would do perfectly as my assistant when I came down to run this show in Pennington. Told me at my own dinner-table. She and Anthea are old school chums, you know.'

'Yes, I do,' she said, seething with resentment at the discovery that Gabriel had got her the job.

'And while we're on the subject, young lady, I take it young Sargent isn't entirely uninterested as far as you're concerned?'

'He's just an acquaintance,' she lied, and gathered up some files. 'I'll get back to work.'

'Not just yet,' he ordered. 'Sit down a minute, Imogen.' She obeyed, looking at him warily. 'How long since your husband died?' he asked bluntly.

'Over a year now.'

'Do you still feel like a widow?'

She stared at him, startled, shocked by the sudden knowledge that she no longer felt like Philip's widow at all. And hadn't done since meeting Gabriel. 'No. I suppose I don't.'

'Good. Take my advice, my dear. We haven't known each other long, but I'm sure you won't take umbrage at a man who's seen a lot of the world. Life is short, and you're a beautiful young woman, so make the most of it.' He coughed loudly. 'And that's enough of that. Anthea would have a fit if she heard me.'

Imogen smiled. 'You're right, of course.'

'I'm never wrong.' His eyes gleamed. 'Well, if I am I never admit it! Now off you go. Take a long lunch-hour for once. Think over what I said. Oh, and by the way,' he added, halting her at the door, 'it's true that I gave you an interview on Sargent's recommendation, but I took you on for one reason only—you were far and away the best candidate for the job!'

*   *   *

Imogen found life very different after the weekend of the second cricket match. Gabriel, as was obvious from that evening when she got home, had decided to embark on a strategy designed to weaken every defence she possessed. Tash met her at the door, smiling all over her face as she pulled her through the kitchen and into the hall. In pride of place on the table under the mirror stood an exquisite arrangement of flowers.

'From Gabriel,' she crowed, handing her the card propped against the delicate porcelain container.

'How do you know?' demanded Imogen, her colour high as she opened the envelope.

'I may be just a naïve little student, unversed in the ways of the world,' said Tash, eyes cast down in mock humility, 'but if Gabriel doesn't fancy you rotten I'm Julia Roberts!'

'Nonsense!' Imogen read the card, biting her lip. 'From Gabriel' was the unembellished message.

'Is he thanking you for supper?' demanded Tash, agog with curiosity.

'Not in so many words. But I suppose that's what he intended.' Imogen made for the stairs. 'I'm off for a bath. What do you want to eat?'

'Supper's ready. Salad again, but I made pasta to go with it. It's a sort of bake, and it's in the oven right now, so hurry up; I'm—'

'Starving!' Imogen finished for her, and laughed. 'Survive for ten minutes and I'm with you.'

Over the meal, which Imogen ate with appetite, much to the young chef's delight, Tash prattled on about her day and how she'd given Sam Harding his coffee, then gone off for a game of tennis with Hector.

'They've got a court at Camden House,' she said, collecting their plates. 'Mrs Sargent's nice, isn't she? Sort of brisk and no-nonsense, but I liked her. She gave us tea and cakes.'

'No wonder you liked her!'

Tash laughed, then set down a dish of sliced fresh peaches and a carton of ice-cream. 'She gave me the peaches, too. From her garden.'

'You were obviously a hit with her.'

'I'd say you were even more so, from the way she talked about you. She asked us to lunch next Sunday— just a family lunch this time—but I told her I was going to Gran's, so she asked us for the following week instead. Can we go?'

'I already owe her a lunch.' Imogen hesitated. 'I'll ask her here instead. Hector too, of course. Does that tie in with Steph's visit?'

'I forgot!' Tash coloured guiltily. 'Mrs Prescott rang today. Steph's got glandular fever so the visit's off. It's catching, so I can't even go and see her.'

'What bad luck,' said Imogen with sympathy, then eyed her stepdaughter as Tash finished her dessert with relish. 'Does that rule out Chris too?'

Tash shrugged, elaborately casual. 'I had a word with him. Said I'd see him when he brings Steph to college—if she's better by then.'

'He could have come to see you without his sister— if you'd wanted him to.'

Tash's big blue eyes opened innocently. 'I didn't think you'd approve—with you out at work all day.'

'Oh, really!' Imogen laughed. 'What about Hector? Doesn't that apply to him too?'

'No fear—Hector's no threat to my virtue.' Tash giggled.

'How can you be sure?'

'He told me—when I mentioned about Chris not coming and so on. Hector's got a healthy respect for his mother's wrath—not to mention his big brother's.'

'Fear of retribution stronger than the natural urges of the libidinous male?' enquired Imogen drily. 'Surely not.'

'He hasn't shown any libidinous urges towards me— yet.' Tash sighed, then leapt to her feet as the phone rang. 'That'll be Hector.'

She disappeared into the hall but came back almost at once, disappointment warring with curiosity in her expressive young face. 'It's for you. Gabriel.'

Imogen coloured at the look in Tash's dancing eyes as she went off to the phone, and closed the kitchen door behind her with emphasis.

'Hello?'

'Imogen? Did you get my flowers?'

'Yes. Thank you. I would have rung to say thanks, but I don't have your number.' She bit her lip, blushing furiously. Now he'd think that she wanted it.

Gabriel promptly gave her his telephone number and repeated it to make sure she had it correctly. 'I meant what I said,' he added.

'Oh?'

'The flowers are just the beginning. Goodnight, darling. Sleep well—'

'Wait,' she said quickly. 'There's something I have to say.'

'*Have* to say?' he repeated, amused. 'Why is this so difficult for you? It's perfectly simple, Imogen.

We're two people with no impediment to talking together, being together—and making love together,' he finished, his voice roughening in a way which made the hairs stand up on the back of her neck.

'Gabriel, don't,' she said fiercely. 'I meant that quite apart from the beautiful flowers I find I'm obliged to thank you for recommending me to Mr Hastings.'

'You wanted a job, he needed an assistant. Two problems solved. Say one little word and I'll solve any others troubling you. If you'd only give in and admit that you want me as much as I want you it would solve quite a few of mine!'

'What would happen when you stopped wanting me, or I stopped wanting you? Not that I'm saying I do,' she added hastily.

'Of course not!' he said cuttingly. 'It would never do to admit you have feelings and desires, would it, Imogen? And as for your question, it's academic. While I live and breathe I'll go on wanting you. Goodnight, darling.'

And before a speechless Imogen could reply Gabriel hung up.

Later she rang Mrs Sargent to ask her to Beech Cottage for the proposed lunch. 'Hector too, of course,' she added.

Claudia Sargent laughed, asked if Imogen was up to feeding someone with Hector's appetite, then accepted the invitation with pleasure. She chatted a few minutes longer, asking how Imogen was enjoying the job, mentioned a spur-of-the-moment trip which she was taking the following weekend to visit her sister in Cornwall, then said goodbye and handed over the telephone to her young son, who was waiting at her elbow to talk to Tash.

Compared with Imogen's limbo-like existence after Philip's death her life became hectic in the extreme, with things hotting up at the bank to the extent that she was glad to leave the shopping to Tash, who displayed a hitherto undiscovered talent for cooking. Every evening a meal of some kind awaited Imogen's return, some dishes more successful than others, but all of them welcome to her after the demands of her day.

Some evenings were enlivened by Hector's presence at the dinner-table. The relationship between the engaging, lanky young man and Natasha was such a relaxed, uncomplicated one that Imogen enjoyed their company, and left them to it when they refused her help, either with preparing or clearing away the meal.

And every evening Gabriel rang. The conversations were never very long, but every one had the same message—he was no longer taking no for an answer on any subject.

'Your brother rings Imogen every night, you know,' Tash informed Hector one evening as the three of them drank coffee in front of the television news. 'And sent those flowers in the hall.'

Hector gazed at Imogen thoughtfully. 'Are you happy with that? I've never seen him like this about a girl before—' He stopped and coloured painfully as he glanced at Tash.

'It's all right,' she assured him. 'I know Imogen was married to my father but that doesn't mean I resent her friendships with other men. Dad would have wanted her to marry again.'

'I don't think Gabe's into marriage exactly,' said Hector, then closed his eyes in anguish, his face bright crimson. 'Oh, hell, I didn't mean—'

'Hector,' said Imogen, laughing, 'I think we'd better talk about something else before you burst a blood vessel.'

Tash was enjoying herself so much at Beech Cottage with Hector to keep her company that Imogen knew she was reluctant to go away for the weekend to her grandparents.

'But don't let on that I am,' said Tash earnestly. 'I wouldn't hurt them for the world. I'll be back on Monday before you get home from work. I told Grandma last night what a little treasure I am about the house for you.'

'Which is the truth,' said Imogen, hugging her. 'I'll miss my au pair when you go back to college.'

Tash returned the hug with interest. 'I meant what I said, you know. I want to see you happy with someone else, Imogen. And Gabriel Sargent's pretty obviously nuts about you. Can't you just—well—have some fun with him, even if you don't want to marry him or anything?'

'I wonder what you mean by fun,' said Imogen, shaking her head. 'And don't explain,' she said quickly. 'You'll probably shock me!'

Imogen was in no hurry to get home that Friday. The house, she knew, would seem empty without Tash. Also it was raining, which meant that she couldn't spend time in the garden, and unless Gabriel rang she was in for an uneventful evening.

She sighed as she drove down the lane towards Beech Cottage. At one time Friday night had been the best night of the week—work over and the weekend to look forward to, probably with some dinner party or a trip to the theatre. But that had been life with Philip. Now that she was alone Friday night was just another night.

When she put away the food she'd bought in her lunch-hour she smiled as she saw the casserole in the fridge. Tash had taken to studying cookery books lately, and this was obviously a recipe from one of them. A tray stood ready on the kitchen table, laid with embroidered cloth, cutlery and china, a small posy in a liqueur glass at one corner. Touched, Imogen heated the chicken casserole, made herself a pot of coffee, then carried the tray through to the sitting-room to eat her supper in front of the most mindless television programme she could find.

As she was finishing the last of the coffee the telephone rang.

'You sound disappointed,' said Gabriel accusingly.

'I thought it was Tash, reporting in from Windsor.'

'Ah, yes—Hector was grumbling about having no one to play with this weekend.' He laughed. 'Mother's left him to cater for himself.'

'Perhaps he'll come up to you if he's at a loose end.'

'No point. I'm away for the weekend.'

She blinked, waiting for him to say where, but he merely told her to take it easy, said goodbye, and rang off. She stared blankly at the telephone as she replaced it. Where was he going? she wondered in fury, annoyed to find herself burning with curiosity. It was no business of hers how Gabriel spent his weekends. Or the rest of his time either, she reminded herself, and went back to the television, feeling deeply dissatisfied with life one way and another.

Half an hour later the phone rang again and she raced to pick it up.

'Tash?'

'No, Imogen. Barbara here. Any idea what time that naughty granddaughter of ours is due? We're getting a bit anxious.'

Imogen stood very still. 'Why, no. I was home late tonight, knowing she was on her way to you. So I don't actually know what time she'll get there.'

'She told us not to meet her at the station—that she'd get a taxi,' said Barbara anxiously. 'But I think I'll get Henry to meet the next train.' She gave a not very successful chuckle. 'I suppose I sound like a hen with one chick—'

'That makes two of us,' Imogen assured her with feeling. 'Tell her to ring me as soon as she gets in, Barbara.'

'Of course, dear. I'm sure she'll be here soon.'

Imogen, frantic with worry by this time, roamed around the house, willing the telephone to ring. Ten minutes later she heard a car draw up in the lane and flew to the kitchen window to see Gabriel striding up the path through the twilit garden. She opened the door, her quizzical smile designed to hide the joy she felt at the sight of him, then her smile died as without a word he took her in his arms and held her close.

'I thought you were in London!' she said, leaning back to look up into his face. 'Where were you phoning from?'

'A garage. I stopped to get petrol. I was having a little joke—wanted to surprise you.'

Imogen tensed as she took in the distraught look on his face. 'What's wrong? You look terrible. Are you ill?'

'Darling, listen.' He bent his cheek to hers. 'When I got in I had a phone call from the John Radcliffe in Oxford—'

'The *hospital*?' She went cold. 'What's happened?'

'They'd been trying to reach me for some time.' His arm tightened round her. 'Hector's there—'

'Oh, no!' Imogen put a hand up to his face. 'He's had an accident on the Harley?'

He nodded, then breathed in deeply. 'He wasn't alone. There was a girl with him, and by the description it's Natasha.'

Imogen freed herself and stood erect, her eyes meeting his. 'Go on, Gabriel. Tell me what happened. I shan't fall apart. Are they both dead?'

He grasped her hands, his haggard face dark with remorse. 'God, no—forgive me, my darling, I should have made that clear right away.' He shook his head. 'I'm not thinking straight. The police said a lorry swerved in front of them on the M40 and they both came off the bike. Tash broke a wrist, Hector's fractured a leg and both are deeply concussed—too much so to answer questions, I gather. Hector had identification on him but Tash didn't. By the description I was able to inform the hospital who she was and told them I'd notify you.'

She nodded, shaking with relief. 'Right. Are you going there now?'

'Of course. I'll take you.'

'You must be tired if you've come from London. I'll drive.'

To her surprise he agreed. 'Right. I'll drive back. Shall we take my car, or would you prefer your own?'

She opted for her own car, then rang Tash's grandparents and gave them what information she could, promising to meet them at the hospital.

'How about your mother?' she asked Gabriel afterwards.

'I won't ring her until I've seen Hector,' he said decisively. 'Not much point in worrying her until I know exactly how he is.'

She nodded. 'Leave it until morning—let her get a night's sleep. I'll just dash up and get a few of Tash's things together, in case there's something she needs.'

When she hurried back into the kitchen she waved a large wallet at Gabriel. 'No wonder Tash had no identification on her. I found this on the floor by her bed.'

He smiled ruefully. 'In too much of a hurry to get off. How does she normally travel?'

'By train.' She shuddered. 'She knew perfectly well I'd have vetoed a trip to Windsor on the back of the Harley.'

'Hector's normally a pretty sensible lad, you know,' said Gabriel in quick defence, and she shook her head.

'I'm not blaming Hector! I'm sure the accident wasn't his fault. Anyway, come *on*, Gabriel. Let's go.'

He took her in his arms. 'I want this first.' He kissed her deeply, hungrily, yet without passion, as though the touch and taste of her fulfilled a deep need, and Imogen responded in kind, holding him close, giving him what he needed in full measure, at the same time taking comfort from the warm, hard haven of his embrace. They drew apart, looked for a moment into each other's eyes, then ran for the car to drive through the wet, gloomy twilight to Oxford.

When they arrived at the hospital Gabriel made enquiries at the reception desk, then took Imogen to find Tash before seeking out Hector.

Tash was awake, looking small and frightened in the accident ward, her face bruised and colourless beneath her tan, her wrist in plaster. Her blue eyes lit up like lamps as she saw Imogen, who sat down on the bed and gathered her into her arms, holding her close as Tash sobbed bitterly against her shoulder.

'How are you, sweetheart?' asked Gabriel gently, and Tash pulled herself together as Imogen mopped her up with tissues.

'I'm OK. I don't really remember much. But never mind me—have you seen Hector? I've been so worried—'

'Gabriel's on his way to him now,' said Imogen firmly, laying Tash back against the pillows. 'He'll come back and report. I'll stay here. No more crying, darling.'

Gabriel stooped to stroke Tash's cheek, then kissed Imogen and went off to find his brother.

'I'm sorry, Imogen,' said Tash in remorse, her eyes enormous in her bruised face. 'Hector suggested taking me to Gran's. He's got a chum in Guildford— he was going to spend the weekend with him, then bring me back again on Monday. Do they know what happened?'

Imogen nodded, assured Tash that everything was taken care of, then went off to consult the night staff, and learned that her stepdaughter would be released the following day if they were satisfied that the concussion was better. She relayed the news to Tash, helped her change into one of her own nightgowns, then went off to find Gabriel, since it was plain that Tash was unlikely to settle until Imogen reported back on Hector's condition.

She was given directions to the ward where Hector, bruised more severely than Tash, lay with one leg in plaster from above the knee. His eyes were heavy with remorse as she reached his bed. Gabriel stood up and gave her his chair, and she took Hector's hand.

'Imogen, I'm so *sorry*—is Tash really all right?' said Hector thickly, and brushed a hand across his eyes. 'God—I can't stop blubbing like a kid.'

'He's only just come round properly,' explained Gabriel.

'Tash is fine. She's just worried about you, so I'll stay a minute then get back to her,' she said, smiling. 'Otherwise she won't get any sleep.'

'Tell her I'm sorry,' said Hector, swallowing. 'I've never had an accident before. One minute we were toddling along in the slow lane, then—wham!—I wake up in here.'

'A lorry swerved in front of you.' Gabriel's jaw tightened. 'You were lucky, old son. It could have been a hell of a sight worse.'

Imogen got up and bent over Hector to give him a gentle kiss. 'Stop worrying, Hector. Tash will be fine—

even better now that I can reassure her you're more
or less in one piece.'

He looked up at her earnestly. 'Tell her—' He licked
dry lips. 'Tell her I wouldn't have had it happen for
the world.'

She squeezed his hand, then left the ward, followed
by Gabriel for a moment.

'They've told me he's fine,' he said in an undertone. 'He just needs rest, and as soon as they're satisfied that the concussion's better I can take him home.
In the meantime I suggest we book in somewhere for
the night. Then we can come and go at the hospital
as we please, without wearing ourselves out with the
drive.'

She nodded. 'Good idea. I'll use some of Tash's
stuff overnight, then buy whatever else I need in the
morning.'

'The Randolph suit you?' he asked.

'Fine.' She smiled at him. 'I'm glad Hector's all
right. Try to convince him he's not to blame for the
accident. While you do that I'll ring the hotel and
book us in.'

Gabriel bent to kiss her swiftly. 'I'll come along
and collect you once Hector's settled for the night.'

When Imogen got back to the ward Tash's grandparents were with her. They both embraced Imogen
with affection, but after only a short time with the
tired girl all three were banished to let the patient sleep.

Barbara and Henry had arranged to stay with
friends in Oxford. Imogen told them that she would
be staying at the Randolph, then kissed them both
goodnight. A moment later Gabriel arrived to say that
Hector was sleeping.

'Well?' he said as they drove into the town. 'How are *you*, my darling?'

'Shattered,' she said unsteadily. 'Poor Hector, he was in such a state about Tash—and she about him. Now that they both know the other's all right I think they'll sleep like logs. Although Hector must be in pain with that leg.'

'He can cope with pain. It was Tash he was in agony about.'

When they arrived at the Randolph Imogen announced them as 'Sargent' very crisply, avoiding Gabriel's eye as the receptionist handed the porter a single key. She was deeply aware of his tension as they followed the man up the wide stairs in silence and waited as he unlocked the door.

Gabriel thanked the porter, tipped him liberally, then followed her inside the room and closed the door, his eyes questioning as they met hers. For answer she held out her arms, and he caught her in a rib-cracking embrace, giving her a smile which turned her heart over in her breast.

'Are you sure?' he demanded huskily.

She nodded and laid her head against his chest. 'I looked at those two young things lying there in hospital and suddenly everything seemed so simple. By the grace of God Tash and Hector weren't killed today. But they could have been—their lives snuffed out between one moment and the next.'

He shuddered and held her so tightly that she feared for her ribs. 'Don't. It must have been a sheer nightmare for you after the way your husband died.'

'Oddly enough I wasn't thinking about Philip,' she admitted with honesty. 'It struck me that what happened to Tash and Hector could happen to anyone, any time. Including you and me. So no more silly pretending that I don't want you as much as you say you want me. Life's too short to waste a minute of it.'

'Imogen,' said Gabriel, in a tone which turned her bones to liquid, 'as well as wanting you, I love you. I couldn't say that before because I suppose I didn't recognise the emotion. It's new to me. I want you right enough. At this moment, just holding you like this, it's something my body can't hide from you. But I like you too. I want to be your friend as well as your lover—all things to you, husband most of all.'

She leaned back to look up into his face. 'Gabriel, I loved Philip, but what I feel for you is different. You know I fought against it, but almost from the first you were the other half of me I didn't even know was missing until I met you.'

She saw his eyes darken and felt his hands shake as they cupped her face. Then his mouth was on hers and suddenly the emotions of the day overtook them. Nothing in the world could have stemmed the cataclysm of desire which overwhelmed them as the agony of worry they'd shared was channelled into a physical union of power and love and thanksgiving to celebrate the sheer joy of being together and alive.

'It won't be easy,' said Imogen, long afterwards when she could speak.

Gabriel made no pretence at misunderstanding. 'Nothing worth having ever is, my darling.' He raised his head to look into her heavy, glittering eyes. 'Say it, Imogen.'

She smiled slowly. 'I thought I had.'

He slid his hands into her tangled hair. 'You haven't. And I won't let you go until you do.'

'I love you, Gabriel Sargent,' she said gruffly.

He let out a great sigh of elation and bent his head to kiss her. 'As long as you love me, Imogen,' he said against her mouth, 'no problems are insurmountable.'

'I live in Abbots Munden, you live in London,' she pointed out, rubbing her cheek against his.

'You could come and work at head office—'

'No. I promised I'd stay with Mr Hastings until he retires.'

Gabriel nodded. 'Whatever you want, Imogen. And I promise you I've got no more secrets or surprises for you—except one.'

He got to his feet, stretching his lean, muscular body with unselfconscious luxury as he went into the bathroom. He returned with a towel knotted about his slim hips, crossed the room to the clothes he'd flung over a chair and took a box from the pocket of his jacket. Then, with a blazing, victorious smile at Imogen, he opened the small refrigerator and took out a bottle of champagne and two glasses.

'Will I like this surprise?' she asked, propping herself against the pillows.

'Yes,' he said simply, and sat on the bed beside her. He poured champagne into a glass, handed it to her, then put the box in her other hand and slid into bed beside her, leaning against the headboard as she flicked open the small leather box with her thumbnail.

Philip had given her a large solitaire diamond—a modern, fabulously expensive ring which she had kept locked away since his death. The exquisite ring in the box was old, Victorian in design, with diamonds and emeralds in a raised claw and crown setting on a wide rose-gold band. Imogen's throat thickened with unshed tears as Gabriel drew off her wedding-ring and slid his replacement on her finger. He raised her hand to his lips and kissed it, then looked into her eyes.

'Will you wear this, Imogen?'

She nodded wordlessly, the champagne glass tilting dangerously in her hand. He laughed unsteadily as he rescued it and put it to her lips.

'A toast. To Natasha and Hector, thank God. And to us.'

Imogen repeated the toast with fervour, drank a little of the champagne, then Gabriel took it from her and drank from the place where her lips had touched.

'To us,' he said again, then drained the glass and put it down so that he could take her in his arms. 'No matter how we arrange our lives, Imogen—whether it's just weekends together at first, or a few snatched hours whenever we can—the time we *are* together will make up for all the hours apart.'

'And what happens when Mr Hastings leaves?' she asked, raising an eyebrow. 'Will you give me a job in London?'

'I was coming to that,' he said, his arms tightening. 'I'd like nothing better than having you for an assistant.' He kissed her thoroughly before going on. 'What man wouldn't?' he said, smoothing her hair back from her damp forehead. 'But I'm going to want more than that. Could you juggle two careers at once, Imogen?'

She pulled away a little, her eyes brilliant with curiosity. 'What did you have in mind?'

'A baby,' he said softly, then grinned at her astonished look. 'And, since you object to my habit of concealing certain facts, perhaps I'd better make it clear right now that I'd like more than one. Subject to your consent, of course.'

'A baby,' she said in wondering tones, as though she'd never heard of one before.

'It's quite usual,' Gabriel pointed out.

She nodded. 'True.' She bit her lip. 'Now that you've brought the subject up it occurs to me that it's sheer luck the question hasn't arisen already.'

He smiled and held her close. 'Now I'm being so honest and up front all the time I'll admit I'd hoped you were pregnant already—from that first night together. It would have been the perfect way to slice through the Gordian knot you insisted on tying us in.'

She pushed him away, eyeing him challengingly. 'Oh, yes? Well, I'm not. At least—' She stopped, colouring.

'At least?' he prompted, his eyes dancing.

'I wasn't before tonight,' she muttered, and with a shout of laughter he crushed her close and kissed her until she was dizzy.

'Would you mind?' he demanded after a while, raising her face with a peremptory finger.

'Not much point,' she said tartly, then her eyes softened as she realised that a trace of anxiety lay behind the demand in his eyes. 'No, darling, I suppose I wouldn't mind at all. After all,' she added, with a sly little smile, 'I'm older than you, so I suppose I'd better get started if I do want to be a mother.'

He shook her a little, his eyes boring into hers. '*Do* you want a baby? Truthfully, Imogen?'

She smiled slowly, and kissed him, returning his embrace with interest as his arms crushed her close. 'Yes,' she said breathlessly. 'But not *a* baby, Gabriel— *your* baby—a little angel just like his father.'

He buried his mouth against her neck. 'I'm no angel, Imogen.'

'Quite the reverse,' she agreed in a stifled voice as he caressed her.

He raised his head to look at her. 'You mean I'm a devil?' he said, eyes glittering.

'No. Just a very earthbound angel—Gabriel!'

ℋarlequin Romance®

Coming Next Month

#3423 MARRYING THE BOSS! Leigh Michaels
All Keir Saunders was interested in was making money, and so when
he needed a wife to complete a business deal, it seemed easiest to buy
one! His secretary, Jessica, was the logical candidate. And though she
was certain matrimony wasn't in her job description—how could she
refuse a man like Keir?

#3424 A SIMPLE TEXAS WEDDING Ruth Jean Dale
It began simply enough when Trace Morgan hired Hope to organize his
sister's engagement party.... But Trace didn't want the wedding to go
ahead. And he certainly didn't want to fall in love with the hired help!

#3425 REBEL IN DISGUISE Lucy Gordon
Holding Out for a Hero
Jane was a cool, calm and collected bank manager. Gil Wakeham was
a rebel. But Jane had accepted his offer of adventure—a summer
spent with Gil and his adorable basset hound, Perry. The dog had
stolen her sandwiches. Was Gil about to steal her heart?

#3426 SOMETHING OLD, SOMETHING NEW Catherine Leigh
Hitched!
Lily Alexander's husband, Saige, had been missing—presumed dead—
for seven long years when he walked back into her life! And though
Lily was overjoyed to see him, the timing was awkward, to say the
least. Lily's wedding to her new fiancé was imminent! But Lily could
hardly marry placid lawyer Randall when her sexy rancher husband
refused to let her go!

AVAILABLE THIS MONTH:

#3419 KIT AND THE COWBOY	**#3421 TEMPORARY TEXAN**
Rebecca Winters	Heather Allison
#3420 EARTHBOUND ANGEL	**#3422 DESPERATELY SEEK-**
Catherine George	**ING ANNIE**
	Patricia Knoll

Harlequin Romance ®

brings you

Some men are worth waiting for!

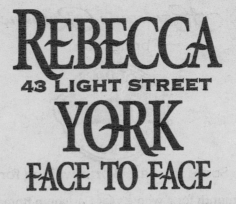

REBECCA

43 LIGHT STREET

YORK

FACE TO FACE

*Bestselling author Rebecca York returns to "43 Light Street"
for an original story of past secrets, deadly deceptions—and
the most intimate betrayal.*

She woke in a hospital—with amnesia…and with child.
According to her rescuer, whose striking face is the last
image she remembers, she's Justine Hollingsworth. But
nothing about her life seems to fit, except for the baby
inside her and Mike Lancer's arms around her. Consumed
by forbidden passion and racked by nameless fear, she
must discover if she is Justine…or the victim of some mind
game. Her life—and her unborn child's—depends on it….

Don't miss *Face To Face*—Available in October, wherever
Harlequin books are sold.

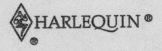

HARLEQUIN ®

®

43FTF

Look us up on-line at: http://www.romance.net

Harlequin Romance ®

brings you

How the West was Wooed!

We've rounded up twelve of our most popular authors, and the result is a whole year of romance, Western style. Every month we'll be bringing you a spirited, independent woman whose heart is about to be lassoed by a rugged, handsome, one-hundred-percent cowboy! Watch for...

- September: #3426 *SOMETHING OLD, SOMETHING NEW*—
  Catherine Leigh

- October: #3428 *WYOMING WEDDING*—
  Barbara McMahon

- November: #3432 *THE COWBOY WANTS A WIFE*—
  Susan Fox

- December: #3437 *A CHRISTMAS WEDDING*—
  Jeanne Allan

Available wherever Harlequin books are sold.

Look us up on-line at: http://www.romance.net

Enter a world where power is everything

POWER GAMES

Coming this August by
New York Times bestselling author

Penny Jordan

Self-made millionaire Bram Soames is a powerful,
charismatic businessman. But he's also a man torn by
guilt over the scandalous relationship that produced
his son.

Jay Soames has always used his father's guilt to keep
anyone from gaining a place in his father's life. Until the
beautiful Taylor Fielding.

Watch as the three of them are drawn into a game they
are powerless to control.

MIRA The brightest star in women's fiction